100 Reasons to Celebrate

We invite you to join us in celebrating Mills & Boon's centenary. Gerald Mills and Charles Boon founded Mills & Boon Limited in 1908 and opened offices in London's Covent Garden. Since then, Mills & Boon has become a hallmark for romantic fiction, recognised around the world.

We're proud of our 100 years of publishing excellence, which wouldn't have been achieved without the loyalty and enthusiasm of our authors and readers.

Thank you!

Each month throughout the year there will be something new and exciting to mark the centenary, so watch for your favourite authors, captivating new stories, special limited edition collections…and more!

Dear Reader

It's a very special thrill to know that this book will be published in such an important and significant year for Mills & Boon. Writing romances for a company that has always been a household name, a company that actually has its title used in the Oxford English Dictionary, has always made me feel so much that I am sharing something that is part of the history of publishing in this country. I'm writing books that are read today just as they were read by the mothers of my readers—and their mothers—their grandmothers—in a tradition that goes right back to 1908. And now, coming right up to date, it means that this latest book of mine is my first published in this very important centenary year.

I first encountered Mills & Boon when I met Marguerite Lees, a friend of my mother who wrote romances for them. As a reader, it was some years before I ever actually read her stories, but as soon as I did I was hooked by great story-telling and fascinating characters—something that I then aimed to bring to my own books when I started out as a writer. It's such a great tradition of telling a great story, creating wonderful characters, and giving the reader the wonderful emotional rollercoaster ride that has always been part of the Mills & Boon story. That's why it was such a thrill when my very first book was bought by them—a thrill that has never lessened right up to today, with the publication of SPANISH BILLIONAIRE, INNOCENT WIFE. I'm so proud to be part of this long tradition—and I hope to stay a part of it for many more years to come.

Happy 100th Birthday, Mills & Boon—here's to the next century of great books.

Kate Walker

SPANISH BILLIONAIRE, INNOCENT WIFE

BY
KATE WALKER

MILLS & BOON™
Pure reading pleasure

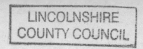
First published in Great Britain 2008
Harlequin Mills & Boon Limited,
Eton House, 18-24 Paradise Road, Richmond, Surrey TW9 1SR

© Kate Walker 2008

ISBN: 978 0 263 86411 3

Set in Times Roman 10¾ on 12¼ pt
01-0308-47455

Printed and bound in Spain
by Litografia Rosés, S.A., Barcelona

Kate Walker was born in Nottinghamshire, but as she grew up in Yorkshire she has always felt that her roots are there. She met her husband at university, and originally worked as a children's librarian, but after the birth of her son she returned to her old childhood love of writing. When she's not working, she divides her time between her family, their three cats, and her interests of embroidery, antiques, film and theatre, and, of course, reading.

You can visit Kate at www.kate-walker.com

Recent titles by the same author:

THE GREEK TYCOON'S UNWILLING WIFE
THE SICILIAN'S RED-HOT REVENGE
SICILIAN HUSBAND, BLACKMAILED BRIDE

CHAPTER ONE

THE hands on the clock didn't seem to have moved even once in all the time that she had been sitting here. Alannah could have sworn that every time she glanced up at the big white circle that hung on the green-painted wall opposite the big hand and the little hand were in exactly the same position as they had been the last time she had looked, making a mockery of the audible sound of the minutes ticking away.

She felt as if she had been here all afternoon—almost all her life. And yet time hardly seemed to have moved on from the moment she had arrived and taken her place in the rather worn armchair in the middle of the room.

From here she could watch the door. She could see the approach of anyone coming near through the clouded pane of glass, and be ready if the door should open and the man she was expecting appeared.

The man she was expecting? Dreading would be more like it, Alannah admitted to herself, green eyes clouding rapidly.

She shook her head so that the red-gold swathe of

her hair tossed along her shoulders, straggling strands escaping from the black elasticated band into which she had confined it before leaving home that morning, and rubbed the back of her hand across her eyes in a vain attempt to drive away the weariness and apprehension that clutched at her.

She knew she looked pale and wan. The stress and sorrow of the past few days had drained every last drop of pink from her cheeks, tears had dimmed the brightness of her eyes and the set of her fine features reflected the strain of the nightmare week she had just endured. The jeans she had pulled on together with a plain black long-sleeved T-shirt, her mind too battered to even think of anything else, did nothing for her appearance. It took even more colour from her skin and left it looking lifeless and washed out. And she hadn't had either the time or the inclination to add any artificial colour with a touch of make-up before she had left her flat. The need to know that her mother was settled at her aunt's house, heavily sedated because of the shock, had been much more important than any personal grooming.

Still, what did that matter? The man she was here to see wouldn't give a damn about her appearance or how she was dressed. He wouldn't want to see her here in the first place and he'd be even less happy about it when he heard what she had to say.

'Of course, Mr Marcín…'

A sudden bustle in the corridor beyond the door alerted her, the sound of the all-too-familiar name confirming her suspicions. Not that she'd needed them confirmed. Whenever and wherever Raul Marcín appeared, it seemed that instantly everything was bustle and activity. Even the air around him appeared enlivened, stirring and swirling in a way that left other more ordinary humans catching their breath in the suddenly rarefied atmosphere.

Once she had been part of that atmosphere, carried along on the tidal wave of energy and power that Don Raul Esteban Marquez Marcín created as he strode through life, arrogant dark head held high, golden eyes blazing. But not any more. Not since she had fled that world and all it brought with it.

And she was well out of it.

It was a world of power and money, yes—but there had also been cold deceit and even icier manipulation. Don Raul Marcín took what he wanted from people—from women—and used them to fulfil his own desires, without a thought for their feelings. He'd done that to her. And he would have discarded her too, she had no doubt. He would have tossed her aside when the purpose she had served was finished—done with. But luckily for her vulnerable heart, and before the foolish emotions she had allowed herself to feel had become so deeply embedded in her spirit that she could have had no hope of ever tearing them out, she had discovered the truth about their relationship. And that truth had set her free. Making her run as far and as fast as she could, never looking back, and never wanting to see Raul Marcín ever again.

Which was how she would have wanted it to stay. Except that now she had no choice. None at all. She had to face Raul Marcín once again. Face him and tell him things she had no doubt that he did not want to hear.

'If you would just wait in here…'

A hand pushed open the door, bringing with it, Alannah would have sworn, a rush of swirling air, and a male voice murmured a word of thanks, although with an edge of impatience on the sound.

Immediately Alannah found that her hands had gone to smooth her hair, straighten her top, and with a mutter of annoyance and reproach she forced them still again. She didn't want him thinking that she wanted to improve her appearance for him; or believing that she was in the least concerned what he would think of her. Once that might have mattered to her; once she might have wanted more than all the world that he would look at her and smile, desire flaring in his eyes—but that had been in the past. Now desire was the last thing she wanted him to feel, so it didn't matter a damn if she was as scruffy and unkempt as some street urchin in a small village on his family's vast estate.

'I'll get that sorted out straight away.'

'*Gracias,*' that voice said again, sending shivers of recognition down Alannah's spine. She wasn't going to let herself feel anything. Not now. Not after all that had happened.

She heard him come into the room, felt his presence in the atmosphere, but still didn't dare bring herself to lift up her head and actually *look* at him. The sudden quiver of awareness that flashed through her body twisted in nerves that were already stretched, turned her natural apprehension into something that was close to a physical pain. It took all her strength to subdue it so that she could only stare at the floor, focusing her gaze on the green and grey pattern of the slightly worn carpet at her feet.

'*Perdón!*'

He had become aware of her silent presence at the far side of the room and out of the corner of her eye she noticed how the tall, lean body stilled, stiffened. She couldn't see his face but there was a quality in his stillness, in that worrying silence, that told her his expression was changing, turning from polite greeting to realisation, to awareness. To…

'Alannah?'

Oh, dear God, but she had forgotten the way his use of her name affected her. That husky accent, the way that just the sound of his voice seemed to coil around her like warm, scented smoke, making her heart clench painfully.

'*Alannah?*'

She had to look at him now. She had no option. It was either that or let him guess just how much he affected her, and that was something she really didn't want him to know.

If she was honest, she'd been taken by surprise at it herself. She'd told herself that she could do this. That she could meet him, face him, tell him what he had to know and then go on her way, back to her life, the life she had built since she'd left him, all over again. She was away from him, she was free and nothing could change that. She was never going back.

But just the softly accented sound of her name on his lips had threatened that conviction disturbingly. She didn't know what it meant, but she was sure as she could be of one thing: she didn't want him to know about it.

'Hello, Raul.'

Trite and inane as it was, it was all that she could manage. And now she had to look at him. It was either that or make it obvious that she was holding back deliberately, that she was trying to do anything but look into his face.

So she lifted her head, forced her drooping eyelids wide open and met his bronze stare head-on.

He was bigger than she remembered. Or, rather, she had forgotten how tall, how strong and imposing he was. And it seemed that the passage of time had only added to the impact he made simply by walking into a room. She couldn't help wishing that she was not sitting down. The armchair was low and squat, making her feel uncomfortably vulnerable as Raul towered over her, overwhelming and ominously threatening.

In the two years since she had seen him, time had turned him from a young man into a dynamic, mature male. His powerful frame had become tauter, stronger, tightening muscles and enhancing his forceful stature. And nowhere were the effects of time on his bone structure more pronounced than in his face. The already lean shape, the high, slanting cheekbones were emphasised by the passage of time that had etched a few lines around his eyes and mouth. His brows seemed darker, thicker, and on either side of the straight slash of a nose his bronze eyes burned like molten gold, fiercely intent on her face.

Unlike her, he was immaculately dressed, the perfectly tailored lines of the elegant steel-grey suit he wore with a crisp white shirt clinging to those honed muscles, broad shoulders and narrow hips as if they had been moulded onto him. That suit and the pristine shirt were so much Don Raul Marcín, she reflected bitterly. So much the Raul she had known in the past. A man she had rarely seen in anything other than those tailored suits, almost never anything casual and relaxed. And his mind-set was the same. Always focused, always business, always working, making money. And when he wasn't working then his attention was on the one other thing that mattered to him—the dukedom of Marquez Marcín and all the land they owned.

'*Buenas tardes Alannah.*' It came stiffly, curtly, with an arrogant inclination of his head, barely acknowledging her and sending stinging pricks of indignation skittering over her skin.

Long time, no see. The flippant words hovered on her tongue but she caught them back, swallowing them down hard, knowing they were not in the least appropriate—nor would they be welcome.

'What are you doing here?'

The harsh demand in his tone drove all other thoughts from her mind, pushing her to her feet in a rush, her hands on the arms of the chair for support.

'The same as you, I presume. This is a hospital.'

'But I…'

The dawn of understanding in those burning eyes eased the sear of them over her skin, making her swallow again as her throat closed up in response to the sight.

'Someone is ill?' It came grimly, sharply. 'One of your family…'

'My brother,' Alannah managed, nodding almost fiercely for fear that he might see what was in her eyes; the tears she was having to blink back hard. She would have to come to the truth soon enough but who could blame her if she needed a little time to draw breath, to prepare herself? Find the courage to go on?

And especially when it was this man she had to tell.

'Is it bad?'

Another change of expression almost defeated her, sweeping away all the strength she had gained. His look of sympathy, of understanding, seemed genuine, so much so that it knocked her sideways, emotionally and physically. She actually staggered where she stood for a moment, uncertain fingers clutching at the chair for support. He looked as if he really cared—though she knew it was only a polite mask, assumed by social necessity. And one that would soon be wiped straight off those handsome features when she explained everything further.

'Bad enough.'

The worst, she should say. But how could she tell him that when admitting what had happened brought with it so many other admissions, so many other complications?

'I'm sorry.'

Raul said it automatically and even though he knew that it sounded cold and distant, his voice harsh, abrupt, he didn't have the energy or the concentration to change it. It wasn't that he didn't feel sympathy for her sick brother, but at this foul end of a long, foul day Alannah was the last person he needed to see right now. The last person he wanted to see now or at any other time.

When she had walked out of his life twenty-five months before, he had been glad to see her go. More than glad. If he had never seen her again, it would have been too soon. He had let her get under his skin in a way that no other woman had ever done before or since. In fact he had come close to wanting to spend his life with her. He had even gone so far as to ask her to marry him.

But when he'd proposed she had laughed in his face.

'Why on earth would I want to *marry* you?' she'd said, her voice showing the scorn that was so clear in the coldness of her eyes, the mocking smile on her lips. 'That's not what I'm in this relationship for. It was fun—and the fact that you're so rich is great. But if you're thinking of anything permanent, forget it! That's just not going to happen.'

And that was when she had told him that she had already met someone else. The wound to his pride still burned like an open sore and her presence here like this had only wrenched away the scar that covered it. Seeing Alannah was the only thing that could make him forget just for a second exactly why he was here at all.

And that he didn't want to forget. If he could have made it that it had never happened then he would, but that was impossible. If he forgot, if he put it out of his mind for a moment, then, inevitably, at some point he had to go through the agony of remembering all over again.

'I'm sorry,' he said again, knowing that, even through the black fury and the hatred of her that had filled his mind since she had walked away from him, if she was going through one quarter of what he was feeling then it was only human to feel sympathy for another person caught in the same horror.

'Thank you.' She sounded almost as unfocused as he felt, but then that was only to be expected if her brother was very ill.

It explained the way she looked, he told himself, his numbed and bruised mind finally registering more about her than the unwanted fact that she was Alannah Redfern, the woman he had never wanted in his life again.

And now that he had become aware of just how she looked, now that his eyes had fixed on her face, he found that he couldn't look away; couldn't drag his eyes from hers.

She looked like a pale reflection of herself, he realised dazedly. It was as if someone had painted her in diluted pastel water colours or left a photograph out in the sunshine until it faded, all the brightness leaching away to leave just a negative of what had been there before.

Whenever a memory of Alannah had slid into his mind—and they had done just occasionally, *maldito sea*, in spite of his determined efforts to lock them out, then those memories had been of colour and life, of a vividly toned and animated face, a wide smile and flashing green eyes.

But now even those eyes seemed faded. The brilliant green that he recalled was dulled to the colour of the sea on a bleak winter's day. Her skin, which had always had the creamy pallor of her Celtic ancestry, was now ashen almost to the point of less transparency where it was stretched tight across the fine bones of her face.

She had lost weight too, he would swear. The lush curves he remembered so well—too well—were lush no longer. Instead she looked finer drawn, almost fragile—and were the long lashes that fringed those almond-shaped eyes spiked by...*tears*?

Tears in a place like this, in a hospital intensive-care ward, were bad news, and with his own terrible revelation still so raw in his mind and his heart he knew that the shadows in her eyes, the lack of colour in her face, were probably mirrored in his.

'Alannah?'

If the look of sympathy earlier had almost destroyed her, then this change in his voice, his expression, took the ground right from under her feet in a second. It was just what she most needed, and yet what she had most been dreading. It was what the weakness deep inside longed for, this note of concern and support, and yet she knew she could never reach for it, never allow herself to lean against his strength, let herself accept his help. Because if she did then she still had to tell him the whole truth. And she knew that if she had once known the feel of that support, even for a second, then it would tear her apart to lose it all over again.

And so she forced herself away from the temptation that had reached out to enclose her, pulling herself away, taking back the two small steps she had taken towards him without even being aware of having moved. She felt the withdrawal in every inch of her, the terrible wrench in her heart as well as her body, and it made her legs tremble beneath her, threatening to give way as she made herself move away instead of towards him and make it look as if she had been heading towards the drinks tray instead.

'Would you like some coffee? It's pretty foul but…'

What was she saying? Offering him coffee one minute and then telling him how foul it was the next! She sounded like… She didn't know what she sounded like, only that the way she was rattling on gave away just how nervous she was feeling and that could only alert Raul to the fact that something was very wrong.

And if he started asking questions…

The nerves in her stomach twisted sharply and painfully, making her heart jump into a rapid uneven beat.

'…coffee, *gracias*.'

At least that was what she thought Raul said but the words were blurred by the pounding of the blood through her veins, sounding like thunder inside her head. And somehow she found that she just couldn't stop talking, no matter how much she wanted to. It was as if, having found a way to remove the gag that had kept her lips tight closed except for the barest minimum of forced speech, she had also ripped away the restraint on her tongue so that the words were just tumbling out in a rush without giving her time to think whether they were really what she wanted to say or not.

'They try to make this place comfortable, make it feel a bit homely, for the families and friends who are visiting—or waiting for news—but of course that's not really possible, is it? I mean, who would want to be *at home* in the families' room of an intensive-care ward?'

The plastic cup she held under the spout of the insulated coffee-pot shook unnervingly in the uncertain grip of a barely controlled hand and she clenched it tighter, only to crush and crack the brittle material.

'Damn, damn, damn!'

Painfully aware of the way that Raul was watching her, of the tall, dark, silently vigilant spectator who stood just behind her, golden eyes intent on every move she made, she tossed aside the broken cup, not caring that it went nowhere near the grey-painted metal bin, and reached for another.

'And who could ever, ever be *comfortable* here? I mean—'

She broke off on a cry of shock and frustration as the too hard pressure on the lid of the coffee-pot forced the hot liquid out at such a rate that it filled the cup in seconds, coming to the rim and pouring over before she had a chance to stop it.

'Oh, *damn* it!'

She knew she should put it down, tried desperately to find a space on the metal tray to do so, but the bitter tears that had been burning at the backs of her eyes now flooded them totally, blurring her vision so that there was no way she could see what to do. If she tried she might miss the tray altogether and so she stood frozen, helplessly unable to decide which way to move.

'Alannah…'

Raul's voice was surprisingly soft and two large, long-fingered hands reached round in front of her. One clamped over her wrist, stilling her and holding her there, while the other eased the sloppy mess of the coffee-filled plastic cup from her now nerveless grip and set it down firmly and securely on the table top. The heat of his body surrounded her, the slightly musky scent of his skin tantalising her senses, and she knew that if she took so much as half a step backwards she would end up hard up against him, feeling the wall of his muscled frame at her back.

'Now,' he said, the beautifully accented voice rasping slightly on the word, 'are you going to tell me just what all this is about?'

'You wanted coffee…'

Did her voice reveal to him, as much as it did to her, just how close to the edge she was? How could he not catch the way it was rough around the edges, as if her control over her words was coming unravelled and all control slipping from her grasp?

'I did *not* want coffee—I have drunk enough of the stuff to float a battleship. And I most definitely do not want any of *that*…'

The hand that had held the plastic cup waved in a gesture of supreme contempt to where it now stood, still filled to the brim with unappealing-looking and rapidly cooling stewed dark coffee.

'But you said…?'

A new wave of panic swept over her as the words and the gesture pulled away her much needed defence of being able to do something—anything—other than actually look him in the face—and, worse, let him see into hers and find the dark secrets she wasn't yet ready to reveal to him.

Had he really said '*No* coffee' and she had been so intent on running away from him, mentally at least, that she had let herself hear the opposite, taking it as the excuse she wanted?

'No coffee…' she managed, having to force her tongue to work.

'No coffee,' Raul echoed emphatically, and the warmth of his breath against her cheek made her shiver in sharp reaction to just how close he was.

She felt as if her skin was afflicted by stinging pins and needles of awareness, prickling all over, lifting every tiny hair on her flesh. Loss and misery were a bitter taste in her mouth, combining brutally with the cruel knowledge that just two years ago, if circumstances such as these had arisen, then Raul would have been the first person she would have turned to, the one she would have known—or at least believed—would be there for her, to help her, support her, lend her his strength, mental and physical, to see her through.

And she would have gone into his arms like a bird seeking its nest, flying straight into their security, thinking that there she would be safe, it would be like coming home, and feeling she could stay there for ever. But harsh reality had taught her that that sense of safety had been false, unbelievable, a total delusion. The truth was that that sanctuary had been, emotionally, the worst place she could have been. The real world, with all its sorrow and bitterness, was still better.

'And now…'

Still caught up in her own unhappy thoughts,

Alannah had no power to resist as the hand that held her wrist tightened, spinning her round to face Raul.

And she was even closer than she had thought. Facing this way, she was almost up against his chest, her nose level with the top button on his shirt, her eyes looking straight at the smooth, bronzed skin of his throat, seeing the way the muscles tensed and released as he swallowed.

'Now you will tell me just what all this is about.'

'All—?'

The words were choked off, the breath snatched from Alannah's lungs as Raul pushed long brown fingers under her chin and lifted it so that her eyes were now forced to meet the burn of his as they bored down into her.

'And before you say "All what?" and tell me that there is nothing wrong, then you should know that I will not believe you.'

How had he known so precisely what she had been about to say? Was he a mind-reader now?

'Why not?'

For a second as his head lowered she thought that he was actually going to touch her, that he might rest his forehead against hers as he had used to do as a gesture of easy affection when they had been together. The thought made her heart clench in panic, her pulse thudding frantically. But he paused just inches away from actual contact and instead clamped his hands over her shoulders, holding her tightly so that she could have no hope of moving away.

'Because I know you and the way you behave…'

'You haven't seen me for two years!'

'Two years is not so long a time—and with someone like you, I would never forget.'

Never forget… So how did she take that?

If her mind were clearer then she might have been able to interpret just how Raul had actually said the words but her thoughts were still buzzing in despair and confusion and she hadn't had a chance to grab at the moment before it was gone again and all she was aware of was the burning stare of those deep-set eyes into her face.

And Raul didn't give her any time to think further.

'I know that however much you try to hide it you are in pieces inside. You are walking and talking like a robot—but *un robot* would at least make some sort of sense and you are making none. And these…'

A hard fingertip brushed lightly over the shadows she knew were under her eyes, traced the lines that stress and sorrow had etched on her face.

'These give too much away. So what is it, Alannah? What has happened to Chris?'

In a series of shocks, it was another she didn't expect. Her head went back in surprise, eyes opening wide.

'Chris… You remember my brother's name?'

'I remember everything,' Raul told her in a voice that shivered all the way down her spine, taking another bit more of her hard-won control with it as it went. 'So now are you going to tell me what has happened? What exactly is wrong with Chris?'

Trapped like a rabbit in the headlights by the burn of those amazing eyes, Alannah felt her grip on what was happening slip and evaporate, leaving her shaking and distraught, a feeling that was worsened by the way that Raul's hands tightened on her shoulders, hard fingers digging into the soft skin under the black T-shirt.

'Tell me,' he said and it was a command, one she knew she disobeyed at her peril. Only the truth would satisfy him and he would know if she told him anything less than that.

'Chris…'

She hunted for a way to say it—but what way was there other than the hard, cold fact that she had been trying to absorb, to accept, to cope with for the past twenty-four hours?

'My brother—Chris's gone…he's dead.'

And as she said that final, dreadful word the last shattered remnants of her control broke completely and the tears that shock had forced back, leaving her unable to mourn, totally overwhelmed her. With no fight left in her, no strength at all, she gave herself up to the misery and the aching, dragging sobs that could not be held back.

Blinded by the tears, she could feel Raul's strong arms come round her, gathering her close, holding her tight, and in the blackness and despair of her loss she had no way of knowing if his gesture was the most wonderful, most welcome thing on earth or if it was the worst, the most dangerous thing that could have happened to her.

She only knew that under her tear-soaked cheeks, against the sudden weakness of her body, there was now the strength and support she needed and so she buried her wet face in the fine material of Raul's jacket and wept her heart out.

CHAPTER TWO

HE SHOULD never have touched her, Raul told himself furiously as he stared out at the lights of the houses flashing past his car as it sped through the darkened streets. He should never, ever have touched her! He should have known just where it would lead.

Maldito sea—what sort of a fool was he? He should have known…

He had let himself believe that two years was a long time. Told himself that in the two dozen months since he had last seen her, since she had walked out of his life without a backward glance, that he had been able to forget her—put her right out of his mind.

Forget her! Hah!

'What?'

Without realising it, he had let the short snarl of bitter laughter escape from his lips as a real sound and the woman slumped beside him on the back seat of the powerful car stirred briefly from the silence into which she had lapsed after the total outpouring of grief and lifted her head to look at him, her eyes just pools of shadow in a white face.

'*Nada*—nothing…' He waved a hand dismissively and she subsided back into silence, head down, preoccupied by her own thoughts.

What was he doing here with her? How had he managed to end up escorting her home like this when he already knew that he had made one of the biggest mistakes of his life in taking her in his arms in the first place? His fingers still stung from where he had touched her skin, the scent of her hair, her body was still in his nostrils in a way that reminded him painfully of the long, burning nights of sexual frustration that he had endured in the weeks after she had left him. Nights that had driven him to seek the company of another woman, any woman, only to find that being with anyone else made the feeling worse, piling dissatisfaction on dissatisfaction until he had felt he would go up in flames because of it.

It was the last thing he should be feeling right now. The last thing he even wanted to think about and yet one touch had put him right back there in the thrall of it. One touch, one moment with her in his arms and it was as if she had never been away.

But what the hell else could he have done? When she had gone to pieces in front of him like that—practically thrown herself into his arms—only a brute would have turned away from her.

Especially when he knew only too damn well just what she was going through, the rawness of grief, the sense of total disbelief that prevented any sort of acceptance.

Lorena.

The beloved name slashed into his thoughts like a stab of pain, making him close his lids sharply against the burn at the backs of his eyes. The thought of the moment that he had had to identify his sister's body, lying cold and still, was a memory that he knew he would never be able to erase.

And with that moment etched so brutally on his mind, and knowing that Alannah was going through something of the same thing, how could he have turned away?

'Thank you for taking me home.'

Having emerged from her withdrawn silence at last, Alannah seemed determined to make herself continue the conversation. Raul could hear the effort she was making to speak in the stiffness of her words, the flat, monotone delivery.

'It's very kind of you.'

Another brusque gesture waved away her words.

'*No es nada,*' he returned, finding it impossible to pitch his voice at anything other than a growl, and he watched her pull her jacket tighter round herself as if she was cold.

'I could have caught the bus.'

Now it was *her* voice that had a distinct chill to it. Every last trace of the woman who had wept in his arms had vanished and in her place was a cool, collected and totally distant female. He could practically feel the ice forming in the car as she spoke. Probably, like him, she was now deeply regretting that she had ever given in to the weak impulse to cry on his shoulder. He need be under no delusion that it meant anything. She had been on the edge of breaking down from the moment he had walked into the room, and he had been the only person there. He had no doubt that if there had been anyone else she could possibly have chosen then she would.

'In this weather?'

This time his gesture indicated the driving rain that was lashing against the car windows, the swish of the hard-working wipers and the splash of tyres through puddles almost drowning his words.

'You would have been drenched before you even made it to the bus stop. Besides, Carlos was waiting to drive me into town anyway and, as we found, we have to go past your flat to reach my hotel.'

And he was not at all prepared to leave her alone on a night like this and in the state she was in. She might have stopped crying, those appallingly harsh, wrenching sobs subsiding slowly into a ragged, gasping near-silence, but her slim body had still been shaking in his arms, her eyes swimming with tears.

'I've done it before.'

'I'm sure you have but with my car available there was no need for you to do it tonight.'

He wondered what she would have done if he had told her that he knew exactly what she was feeling. That he was going through the same hateful experience himself and because of that he'd known he couldn't let her face even the short journey alone.

When a sudden vicious memory of just why he was using her company to keep the darkness from his own thoughts, why he needed her presence to fill the emptiness he was feeling forced itself past the temporary barrier he had tried to erect in his mind, he shook his head roughly, needing to drive away the desperately unwanted images.

'I could have managed!'

Alannah's tone told him that she had seen the abrupt movement and misinterpreted the reason for it.

'I'm not always a wreck like this! I can usually cope—it's just that tonight things—got on top of me.'

'Believe me, I understand. But was there no one else who could have been there with you? Your mother perhaps?'

'My mother is in a far worse state than I am.'

Her voice was low and she was staring out of the window, assuming an intense interest in the passing cars as she spoke.

'It goes against everything in nature for a mother to hear of the death of her child and she has barely recovered from losing my father. She's in pieces—can't sleep…won't eat.'

She shook her head, her mouth twisting, fighting, he knew, against more tears.

'The only way she can cope is with the help of the sedatives the doctor prescribed. At least they knocked her out tonight. But she can't manage anything practical. Everything that has to be done is up to me.'

There was a terrible, raw edge on that last sentence, one Raul recognised only too well. The memory of how she had looked in that hospital room, so lost and alone, with no one there to help her, no support, no company, sent a wave of cold anger running through him.

'So where the hell was *he*?'

That brought her head up, shadowed eyes meeting his sharply.

'Where was—who?'

'The man in your life…'

The man she had left him for.

'Your lover—your boyfriend—whatever you call him.'

'Oh…'

Realisation dawned slowly on Alannah's numbed brain. He was talking about the man she had claimed to be leaving him for. A man who had never existed and still didn't. A man she had totally invented, and she had never met anyone with even half a chance of turning that claim into a reality. How could she have let a new man into her life when she had never fully recovered from the old one?

She'd tried. Since she'd found out just what he really wanted from her and been forced to recognise that her dreams of being loved and cherished to the end of her days were just that—dreams and delusions—she had tried to turn her life around and move on without the happy future with Raul Marcín in it.

But she hadn't succeeded. The few dates she'd been on had been miserable failures, no man seemed to spark even a flicker of the interest and excitement Raul had been able to create just by existing. So just lately she had determined to concentrate on her career and put all thoughts of a romantic life out of her mind. She would have liked to put all thoughts of Raul out of her head too, but her older brother's own new-found romance had made that impossible.

And now the tragic conclusion of that fledgling love affair had brought Raul himself back into her life. The slashing anguish of that thought made her flinch in pain. Would she ever be able to think of Chris again without this terrible rush of agony, the burn of tears?

'Well, at least you're not coming up with some excuse for him.'

Raul had misinterpreted the reason for her silence, thinking it was because of his question about her supposed new partner.

'There's no need for an excuse.' She flung the words at him before she had time to think if they were wise or not.

'No? If you were mine, I would not leave you to handle all this on your own. I would be at your side, every moment of the day.'

'But I'm not yours, am I, Raul?'

And she never had been his, not truly his. Not in the way she had most wanted, most longed to be. Of course he had seen her as *his*. In his mind she had been his woman, his possession, to do with as he pleased. Because no thought of love had ever entered his mind, he had never considered that she might need more than the little he was prepared to offer her.

She couldn't allow herself to think of how much it would mean to have a man like him, powerful, determined and so capable, by her side in these dark, desperate days. A man who would help her, support her. Whose strength would be used for her good, to ease her path as much as he could. There was no point in even letting herself dream of it. That man would never be Raul and he would never be there for her, her actions two years before had made sure of that. It was even more foolish, even more soul-destroying to allow the thought that perhaps as her husband he might have taken on that supporting role. But he would never have been the husband she had dreamed of having.

And the savage truth was that if she had married him then this weekend's tragedy would never have happened and she would never have been in this desperate need of support from anyone.

'And not everyone is a millionaire who can be where he wants to be for as long as he wants to be at the drop of a hat.' Memory made her voice bitter. 'Someone who doesn't have to worry about taking time off work or leaving other commitments…'

The sudden sharp reminder by her conscience of just why Raul was here now, why he had had to drop everything and come to England had her choking off her words and swallowing them down in a rush. She was supposed to have told him the truth about what had happened. That was why she had been waiting for him at the hospital. She had been there to tell him; to make sure that he knew before he found out in any other way. She had to be the one who explained things to him.

But instead she had messed everything up. When she had tried to talk about Chris she had just broken down, gone to pieces, and everything that needed to be said had been left unspoken.

And she could hardly tell him now. Not here, in the darkness of the car, with his chauffeur in the driving seat and the glass panel between him and his passengers in the back partly open so that he would hear every word she said.

'So he is at work, this new man of yours?'

She couldn't answer that, not without lying, and so she hedged her bets, sticking instead to a round-about answer that she prayed would satisfy him without actually coming out with the truth.

'New? It's been two years.'

'So long…and yet you wear no ring.'

It was dropped softly, almost lightly into the silence and Alannah was surprised to find that her instinctive response was to clamp her right hand down on top of her left, pushing the ringless finger out of sight. She didn't know why she reacted in that way, only that some note in Raul's voice had suddenly made a sensation like the slither of something cold and nasty slide down her spine, so that she shifted uncomfortably in her seat.

'There's no need for that.'

Again she dodged round a real answer. There was no need for a ring—but because there was no other man, new or not, in her life.

'Oh, I see—so was that my mistake?'

'Mistake?' Alannah blinked in confusion. Raul Marcín never admitted to mistakes.

'My approach was too conventional? You should have said that you weren't interested in marriage.'

'I wasn't interested in marriage to *you*!'

How she wished it was as convincing as she made it sound. The bitter truth was that she had thought that her heart would burst with joy when he had proposed. It had simply never occurred to her innocent, naïve twenty-one-year-old self that this devastating, sexy man could actually want to marry her for any reason other than that he had been as head-over-heels in love with her as she was with him.

It had truly never occurred to her that a sophisticated man of the world like Raul might have other, more pragmatic reasons for wanting to marry her. Reasons for which her innocence, sexually at least, and her family background were much more important than any feelings she might have.

'It really was just as well we split up when we did,' she said hastily, as much to distract herself from her own foolish thoughts as to fill the awkward silence that had fallen between them. 'After all, what is it they say about repenting at leisure?'

'But that saying is usually preceded by the line "Marry in haste",' Raul drawled mockingly. 'We never actually got that far.'

'And for that we ought to be thankful. If we had got married, it would have been a disaster.'

'You think so?' A sceptical note on the question caught on a raw edge on her nerves.

'Very definitely,' she stated emphatically. 'Don't you agree?'

His sudden silence, his total stillness was unnerving.

Turning to him in confusion, she caught a look she couldn't begin to interpret in his eyes, flashing on and off, on and off as the streetlights caught them and then moved on.

In spite of herself, her heart gave a sudden rough kick inside her chest, making her blood throb in her veins.

He would only have to move a couple of inches, she told herself hazily. He would only have to turn in his seat, just so, and he would be facing her, his head directly above hers. And with her face turned up towards him as it was, then he would just have to lower that proud dark head in order to crush her lips in the kiss he so obviously wanted to take from her. The kiss that the gleam in his eyes, the softening of the beautiful, hard mouth promised.

And the kiss she so wanted from him.

The realisation was like a blow landing on her ribcage, making her catch her breath in shock and confusion.

She wanted Raul to kiss her. Wanted it so much that it was like a scream in her head. But a scream of need that warred in the same instant with an equally desperate scream of denial and warning. This didn't make any sort of sense. It was not only stupid, but it was also dangerous as hell. She should be running miles away from Raul, as far and as fast as she could. Not sitting here, imagining, waiting—yearning…

'Raul…' she said, trying desperately to make it sound like a warning, as offputting as possible. But she had so little control over her tongue that instead it came out on a sensual husk, enticing and provocative when she was trying for exactly the opposite.

'Alannah…' Raul murmured and his tone echoed hers almost exactly, the gravelly purr seeming to coil around her head like perfumed smoke until she felt as if her senses were swimming from just breathing in. And what breath she managed seemed to catch in her throat so that her lips parted on a small, faintly gasping sigh as she fought for control.

Those gleaming eyes were fixed on her and she saw the faint twitch of his mouth into a tiny smile before he sobered again. Staring intently at her partly open mouth. And she could only watch, frozen as his dark head tilted slightly to one side, lowered…

And stopped dead as the car drew in to the side of the road and pulled up, coming to a smooth halt right outside the main door to the building where her flat was. A comment from the driver—something on the lines of 'We're here' in Spanish, Alannah presumed—broke into the taut, heated silence that gripped the two of them as the engine slowed, stilled…

And still Raul didn't move. Still he kept his hooded gaze fixed on her lips, so fiercely intent that she could almost feel its burn along the delicate skin of her mouth, drying them, drying her throat until the sensation became totally unbearable and she had to slick her tongue over her lips to ease the parched discomfort there.

And almost groaned aloud—but whether in relief or disappointment she was unable to say—when she saw how the tiny, brief movement shattered the mesmeric mood. Raul's head came up again, his eyes clashed with hers just for a moment, then glanced away again, looking out into the rain-swept street.

'My stop, I think,' Alannah managed, her voice coming and going on the words like a badly tuned radio. 'This is where I get out.'

If she expected any response, she didn't get one. Instead Raul leaned across her and pushed open the door, letting in a waft of cold, wet air as he did so, then sat back, obviously expecting her to take herself off, out of the car, and as speedily as possible if his closed, withdrawn expression was anything to go by.

'Thank you for the lift.'

'You're welcome.' He made it sound the exact opposite.

The abrupt change from fiercely intent sensuality to cold distance was so disconcerting that Alannah actually felt herself shaking, unable to quite get a grip on herself. She had been so sure…and yet now his mood was so totally different that she was forced to wonder if she had been imagining things, deluding herself completely.

She couldn't get out fast enough, pushing awkwardly and inelegantly out of the car. It was only as she set foot on the pavement, buffeted uncomfortably by the force of the wind and the rain, her short jacket no protection against the inclement weather, that she suddenly remembered in a devastating rush just why she had met up with Raul at all. Why she had been at the hospital in the first place.

She had been there to tell him everything—the whole truth about the terrible accident that had claimed Chris's life—and she hadn't even begun to say anything. She had let the time in the car slide away from her, caught in her memories of the past, in anything and everything other than what she should have been thinking of.

What she should have told him.

What she still had to tell him.

She couldn't let someone else break the truth to him; couldn't let him find out in any other way. There was only one person who could tell him everything that had happened—and it was her duty to make sure he got the right story. It was the last thing she could do for her brother—the only way to preserve Chris's memory.

But there was no way she could turn round now and tell him. What was she to do? Get back in the car and say—'Hang on, I've got something to tell you'? Or say it baldly and bluntly standing here like this, leaning in at the door, where the driver and possibly anyone passing by might also be able to hear.

She couldn't do that to him. Not even to Señor Heartless Raul Marcín. In these circumstances she owed him a bit more than that.

And so she drew on all her strength, took a deep, calming breath, and bent down to lean in at the car door again.

'We don't have to leave it like this, do we? Would you like to come inside—for coffee?'

She knew the form of her words was a mistake even as they left her tongue but she only knew how bad an error she had made when she heard them fall into the silence of the night, sounding horribly light considering the impetus behind them. She felt even worse when she saw the way that Raul's face changed, his eyes narrowing in his shadowed face, his mouth thinning out to just a hard, cold line.

'Coffee?' he said, making the word sound like a curse, as if the drink was a totally alien substance to him.

'Well, you never got a drink in the hospital…' she managed jerkily, seeing no change in that distant expression, no lightening of the darkness of his eyes.

He was going to refuse; she knew it in her heart. He was just a second away from lifting a hand to dismiss her, snapping an order at Carlos to drive on, before pulling the door shut right in her face. And if he did that then she had no way of getting in touch with him again. After all, that was why she had been waiting at the hospital in the first place.

'Please…' she said hastily. 'It needn't be for long. I just want to thank you…'

'No thanks are necessary.'

But then just for a moment he hesitated, looked deep into her eyes. And the narrow-eyed assessment in his gaze made her flinch back away from it as if from some dangerous, poison-tipped arrow. Just what was going through that cold, calculating mind of his?

Then abruptly he leaned forward in his seat, directing some terse command in Spanish to the driver, who glanced at him once, briefly, then nodded.

'What…?' Alannah began then froze as she saw one strong, tanned hand move to unclip his seat belt and toss it aside.

'Half an hour,' he said curtly, flicking a glance at the slim gold watch on his wrist, and then away again. 'Be here at nine,' he told Carlos, the emphatic use of English deliberate, Alannah felt, to get the point home to her. 'And don't be late.'

Could he make it any plainer that he had little time to spare for her, and that he wanted to be away from here as quickly as possible? Alannah asked herself. But at least he was coming. Once they were alone in her flat, in privacy, she would tell him what she had to say as quickly as possible. At least then, with what she felt was her duty done, she would be able to relax.

And Raul would go out of her life again and leave her in peace.

Which was what she wanted most in all the world, she told herself, refusing to let her mind even acknowledge the way that the words suddenly had a disturbingly hollow ring inside her head.

For now, she had enough to cope with just considering what was ahead of her and the prospect of facing the apocalyptic storm that would erupt when Raul knew the truth.

If she could get through the next thirty minutes then her life would be her own again.

CHAPTER THREE

THIRTY minutes and he was out of here, Raul told himself as the lift that was taking them to Alannah's flat sped upwards towards the fifth floor. Less than thirty. He had told Carlos to be back exactly thirty minutes after he had left the car and already more than a couple of those had passed.

Not enough in Raul's opinion. The sooner he got this—whatever this was—over and done with and was on his way again, the better.

The truth was that he didn't know what the hell he was doing here at all. If he had any sense he would have stayed in the car and ignored Alannah's invitation but tonight it seemed that all sense had deserted him, left behind in the headlong rush from Spain after the first phone call alerting him to the news of the accident.

At first he'd thought that the car had come to a halt just in time to stop him from doing something very stupid. The temptation to kiss Alannah, to feel the softness of her lips, taste the intimate flavour of her mouth, had almost overcome him. Another couple of seconds and he would have been lost in the sensual temptation of that upturned face, the soft swell of her lips, the sweet scent of her skin so close to him in the back of the car. So the feel of the vehicle drawing to a halt and Carlos's announcement that they had arrived had come at just the right moment.

But then she'd turned on her way out of the car and looked back inside. Already the steady downpour of the rain had soaked into her hair, making it hang around her face in dripping strands, and drawing attention once more to how pale she was, how huge and dark her eyes appeared above the almost colourless cheeks. He remembered how slender she'd felt in his arms, how fragile, and when she'd suddenly offered him coffee he had found that the instant refusal that had risen to his lips had shrivelled there, unspoken, in the face of the look in those big green eyes.

In that moment he'd thought he understood just why she had asked him to come in with her. He felt he knew just what was in her mind because the same dark feeling, the same dread of being alone with his thoughts was the one that shadowed his own existence.

Because what was waiting for him when he got to the hotel? An empty, soulless room. A mini-bar that in the mood he was in would be far too tempting—but raiding it would not be in the least bit sensible. And he still wasn't sure that he should leave Alannah on her own. She had calmed down since that emotional breakdown back at the hospital, but she was still barely holding herself together. He could see it in her eyes, hear it in the tremor of her voice. And knowing the dark, dragging ache of loss that was always there, he could imagine how she was feeling in spite of her obvious efforts to cover it up.

And so he had gone with her, determined to see her to her flat, to drink that damn cup of coffee. He would delay—for her and for himself—the moment of being alone, the time when the darkness closed around him all over again, hold it back for just thirty minutes, and then leave again. It would still be waiting for him when he came out. Nothing in the world could change that.

'You still live in the same apartment?'

Courtesy insisted that he say something. It was either that or stare at her in stony silence all the way up to her flat.

'The same building.' Alannah was clearly making as much effort as him to make conversation. 'The same floor, in fact. But not the same flat.'

Her tone was low, coolly distant and withdrawn. It was the voice of a stranger, someone he did not know. There was not a trace in it of the ardent, passionate girl he had once known or even of the sweet innocent he had first met. The sweet innocent he had believed she was when they had first met, he corrected himself harshly. He had only seen what he wanted to see and had been pretty quickly disillusioned.

At twenty-one, and fresh from university, she had just been looking for a holiday fling. Mission accomplished, she had moved on to someone else.

'A bigger flat became vacant last year, so I grabbed at it.'

'Room for two.'

'What?'

A puzzled frown drew her arched brows together.

'Your new man,' Raul explained. 'I assume you wanted to move in together.'

'Oh—no, nothing like that.'

A wave of her hand dismissed the man in her life of as little importance as he had been.

'I had a promotion at work and the flat came empty in the same month. I'd always wanted more space, so it seemed the perfect opportunity.'

The lift came to a halt as she spoke, metal door sliding open, and she walked out into the corridor.

'That used to be where I lived…'

Another wave of her hand indicated a door to her left.

'But now I'm down here…'

If she expected a response she didn't get one, other than a quick, inarticulate sound that might have been agreement. From the moment that she had turned to walk away from him, Raul had found that his attention was momentarily distracted. Following Alannah down the blue-carpeted corridor towards the door of her apartment was a sensual experience strong enough to draw his attention completely. The fall of her red-gold hair mirrored the straight line of her back in contrast to the rounded curves of her hips. Long, slender legs in the tight-fitting jeans added to the delight.

He welcomed the sensations, the warmth that flooded his body. It was something to fill the black, empty spaces that seemed to have invaded his heart and his mind ever since he had answered the phone in the middle of the night and heard the news about Lorena's accident. From that moment he felt as if he had been barely moving, speaking, functioning. Even the discovery of Alannah's presence in the hospital room had hardly touched him.

Even when he had held her as she sobbed in his arms, he had felt as if his head was flooded with dark, icy water so that he couldn't feel, couldn't think. He had responded as he would do to any human being who was in pain and distress, and in the same way he had offered her a lift to her flat, taken her out to the car. Because it was the only thing that he could do.

But then there had come that moment in the car, in the darkness of the night, when, looking down into her upturned face as he saw it in the light of the street lamps as they flashed by, he had seen not just another human being but a woman. A living, breathing, beautiful woman.

And that was when he had first felt the stirring of something else, something warmer, something more like a feeling. Something that made him feel as if the black, icy water that filled his thoughts might actually be shot through with tiny rays of light, warming it faintly. But that was when the car had come to a halt, bringing him back to the reality of a cold, dark, wet night in England instead of the warmth of the sun he had left behind in Spain, reminding him of why he was here. And it had brought all the emptiness rushing back.

And when she had got out of the car, paused to look back in, he had seen the same emptiness in her face. And he had known that at least he shared this with her. They might never be close again—hell, they had never truly been *close*—but right here, tonight, they shared this terrible sense of loss. That was when he had decided that for just half an hour, thirty short minutes, they could hold back the darkness together and then go on their way, like ships that passed in the night.

'Come in…'

Lost in his thoughts, he hadn't been aware of the fact that Alannah had opened the door and was now standing with it wide open, waiting for him to walk into her flat.

In an almost colourless face, the deep green eyes were like dark, mossy pools, bottomless and unfathomable, and the pallor of her skin was heightened by the rich fall of her hair, darkened by the rain outside. The same rain that had made the black T-shirt cling to the firm swell of her breasts under the damp cotton.

'You should get out of those wet clothes,' he said, hearing his voice rasp on the words as the bleakness of his thoughts showed in his speech.

He saw the shock that widened her eyes, the deep green flaring suddenly, gold burning in the darkness, and carefully adjusted his tone a degree or two.

'Or at least dry your hair.'

'I'm fine.'

As if to prove it she tossed back the damp strands of her hair and shrugged out of her jacket, dropping it on a nearby chair before heading across the room to where a door stood open into the kitchen.

'And I should make you that coffee.'

Raul's dismissal in his native Spanish was terse and to the point. There was a tension about her slender body that reminded him of a suspicion that had flashed through his mind in the moment she had first invited him in. She was edgy and uneasy, her mood communicating that there was more to this than met the eye. She didn't really think that he believed she had brought him up here for *coffee*?

Just coffee wouldn't put the ragged edge to her voice, make some unreadable emotion darken her eyes.

But she was obviously going to ignore him as she turned and headed through the door into the kitchen.

'Bathroom,' he said sharply, making her stop so abruptly that it was almost as if she had been expecting him to speak.

But obviously not what he had said, he realised as she frowned faintly in some confusion.

'Where is your bathroom?' he repeated.

'Oh—down the corridor…' She pointed in the right direction. 'First door on the left.'

It took him just moments to stride down the corridor, enter the bathroom and snatch up the towel that was hanging on a rail against the wall. With the soft white cotton dangling from his fingers, he was back in the kitchen while she was still filling the kettle at the tap.

'Here…'

With one hand he removed the still dripping kettle from her grip and set it down on the worktop. With the other, he draped the towel over her head and began to gently blot the soaking strands of her hair.

Alannah froze. Every inch of her slim frame became stiff with tension and rejection.

'*What* are you doing?' she demanded from under the towel.

'I should have thought that was obvious. I'm drying your hair.'

'Then stop!'

It came from between gritted teeth, venom in every word. Enough to freeze his hands, still holding the towel.

'I never asked you to do that—or anything like it. I said I was fine.'

'You don't look fine—'

'I'm *fine*—so take your hands off me.'

'Sure!'

Raul's tone was clipped and hard. He dropped the towel on the floor and took a step backwards, hands coming up between them, bronzed fingers splayed wide in what looked like a defensive gesture.

But the expression in his eyes made a nonsense of any thought of defensiveness. There was nothing wary or unsure in the gaze that clashed with her. Instead a cold anger turned those burning bronze eyes translucent and challenge blazed out of them, defying her to take this further.

'But in the terms of strict accuracy, my hands were never *on* you. So it seems that you, Alannah *querida*, are exaggerating just a little. More than a little.'

'I'm…' Alannah began but Raul ignored her attempt to protest, or apologise—she wasn't quite sure which—and when he ploughed straight on, talking right over what she had been about to say, she found she was grateful that she hadn't got so far as the apology.

'If I had touched you then you might have something to complain about. Or if I'd kissed you…'

Alannah saw his intent in those devastating eyes, saw the way his head tilted, his gaze going to her partly open mouth.

'You wouldn't…'

She wanted to run—to get away—but even as the thought came into her mind she knew that he had got there first. Any chance of escape was cut off as one strong hand came down on the edge of the sink on either side of her body, enclosing her, trapping her and holding her unable to move.

He was so close—too close—and all the disturbing, worrying sensations that had sprung to life in the car now flared through her again but this time more sharply, more intensely, making her shift uncomfortably in the confined space of his imprisoning arms. But that only brought her up close against their warmth, their strength, and the hard, lean length of his body in front of her. Her heart was racing, sending blood pounding through her veins, and the sound of it was like thunder inside her head.

He was going to kiss her, she could be in no doubt at all about that. It was there in the smokiness of his gaze, the total stillness of his powerful body. He was going to kiss her and this time there would be no sudden stopping of the car, no announcement from Carlos to distract him from his purpose.

Nervously she slicked her tongue over dry lips, waited, watched as his handsome face came nearer…

And stared in disbelief as this time he was the one

who called a halt, the slow movement stopping, his dark head moving in a gesture of denial.

'I think not,' he said harshly and spun on his heel, turning to march out of the door, leaving her staring blankly after him, wondering just what she had done to change his mind.

Was it some small reaction she couldn't control? Had he seen something in her face? What—just *what* had stopped him, changing his mood and driving him away from her like that?

'Raul…'

She tried for his name but the sound died in her mouth, shrivelling on her tongue. And she was only talking to his back, the long, straight line of his spine, the proud set of his dark head that was all she could see as he walked away from her. If he heard her at all then he made no sign.

And to Alannah's shaken consternation that made her feel terrible, stunned and bewildered, shaking in reaction, and with her legs suddenly unsteady beneath her.

He might as well have kissed her; she was reacting as if he had. If he had actually wrenched her into his arms, plundered her mouth with his, ravaged her senses, he could not have made her feel any worse than she did now—or did she mean that she might actually have felt better? Shaking her head bemusedly, Alannah admitted to herself that she didn't know. She only knew that she was trembling with reaction to just the closeness, the burn of the heat from his body along her senses. Her skin had prickled as if under assault from sensual pins and needles, her nerves twisting tight in anticipation of his kiss and then there had been the terrible sense of let-down when it hadn't happened.

Let-down.

Even in her own thoughts, the word sounded wrong.

She had spent the last two years putting her time with Raul Marcín behind her, determined to forget about it, get him out of her life for good. She didn't want to remember him, didn't want to be with him, didn't want him to have any part in her life, she told herself as she grabbed at the kettle again and shoved it fiercely under the tap. She could only feel thankful that Raul was no longer in the room to see the way that her jerky, clumsy movements betrayed her, giving away the unsettled way she was feeling, the conflict that was raging inside her.

'Oh, no—no!' The words slipped from Alannah's lips, hidden under the rush of water as she turned on the tap to fill the kettle. 'No—it can't be this way!'

But she had loved him once and what was it that they said—that you never forgot your first love? She had adored him, fallen hopelessly, helplessly, irredeemably in love with him in the space of a heartbeat and she had put her own foolish, vulnerable, naïve and *innocent* heart into his hands and his keeping, only to have him crush it brutally, tearing it into pieces. But at the same time, in the way that long ago dinosaurs left their footprints etched into stone, so he had left his mark on her and her senses, her memories, had responded to his touch, his closeness at the most basic, most primitive level of awareness.

She made a terrible, a stupid mistake in the hospital

when, weak and despairing, she had flung herself into his arms and sobbed out her misery on his shoulder. She'd allowed herself to know, just for a very short time, the dangerous, the forbidden comfort of having his arms around her, his strength supporting her, the lean power of his body close to hers. And doing that had weakened her defences, opened cracks in the armour she had built up around herself so that something about Raul could get through to her and stab at her cruelly, leaving her more vulnerable to him than she had been before.

So when he'd tried to dry her hair she'd reacted—overreacted—like a scalded wildcat, turning on him hissing and spitting, so that she had only herself to blame for his cold anger, the way he had walked out on her. And by being overly defensive she had given away too much of the vulnerability she was really feeling.

But not again, she determined as she slammed the lid onto the kettle before banging it down on the stove; never, ever again.

'If that is for the damned coffee you seem so insistent on, then I have to say yet again that I really do not want one.'

Raul had appeared in the doorway again, big, dark and dangerous-looking, a disturbing scowl on his face.

'Then what do you want?'

His broad shoulders lifted in an expressive shrug, but even though the gesture seemed to dismiss her question as irrelevant something new flared in the deep bronze pools of his eyes. Something that sent a shiver of apprehension skittering down her spine as she realised that her uneasiness had caught on his nerves and what she saw in his gaze was coldly burning suspicion.

'You tell me—after all, you were the one who invited me in. And coffee was your excuse for doing so.'

'It wasn't an excuse…'

The knowledge of why she had really invited him into her flat, the worry that she still hadn't dared to broach the subject, made her voice croak in a way that she knew sounded as if she had something to hide.

'No?' Raul questioned harshly. 'Then why am I here? Because you will not convince me that *coffee* was uppermost in your mind.'

'Not *uppermost*,' Alannah conceded but then she saw the way that his head went back, his eyes narrowing, and her throat closed up sharply, preventing her from going any further.

'*Sí?*' Raul questioned sharply. 'So if the coffee was not the most important thing—then what was? Tell me why I am here—why you invited me to your flat in the first place.'

Pushing a hand into his jacket pocket, he pulled out a slim black mobile phone and held it up between them.

'And tell me the truth or I will call Carlos and tell him to come now…'

His thumb moved, hovered over the speed-dial button.

'No—wait…'

She couldn't let him go, not until she had told him the truth that he had demanded—the truth about Chris and the accident and… But how could she tell him without carefully leading up to it? She couldn't just blurt it all out, throw it in his face without any lead-in or preparation. That was why she had made such a fuss about the coffee.

But where could she start? How could she tell him when she knew already just what his reaction would be?

She should start with Chris…but just the thought of the name of her adored younger brother made her mind freeze in pain, unable to frame a single word but *Chris*.

'Alannah…'

She had waited too long, her thoughts preoccupied by her worries, and Raul was growing impatient, his use of her name a low growl of warning. As she forced herself to focus she saw his thumb move again, threatening to press the button.

'No—please wait!'

To her intense relief he hesitated, stopped the movement, his thumb barely a centimetre above the surface of his phone. The bronze eyes he turned on her seemed to burn over her skin, searing away a fine layer and leaving her feeling raw and exposed, desperately apprehensive.

'Then tell me.'

'I will—I promise. But not here. Not like this. Why don't we go and sit down? We'd be more comfortable in the living room.'

But comfortable for how long? She had to tell him now; had to get it out in the open or he would walk out before she managed it. But she didn't dare to think of what would happen after she'd told him. Deep in the pit of her stomach all the nerves twisted into tight, cruel knots of trepidation until she felt that she might almost be sick.

'I need to be comfortable for this?'

That note of suspicion had deepened, darkened, intensifying all her fears just to hear it.

'It would be more—more civilised. Look, just give me a minute to get a drink, a glass of water—you might not want one but I do. And then I'll—then we can talk.'

For an uncomfortable second she thought he was going to refuse. The cynical, sceptical glance he turned on her face made her stomach muscles tighten in apprehension. But then, just when she thought he wouldn't, he inclined his dark head in agreement.

'OK,' he said as he turned and walked back into the living room. 'I will wait—but only a minute. I am not a patient man and I want to know just what the hell is going on.'

Left behind, Alannah snatched up a glass and shoved it under the tap, splashing cold water into it until it spilled over, flooding down the sides and over her fingers. Wrenching off the tap with one hand, she lifted the drink to her mouth and took several long, thirsty gulps of the cool liquid then lifted it to her forehead, rolling the wet glass above her eyebrows in an effort to calm herself down, ease the tension that was already tight as a steel band around her skull.

She had to get a grip on herself. She had to go in there and talk to him as calmly as possible—tell him everything that had happened and then…

She winced inside as she anticipated Raul's probable reaction, the dark thunderstorm that would probably break right over her head as soon as she finished speaking. But it had to be done—and soon too. Thirty minutes, he had said, and they had already used up more than half of those. If she didn't hurry then Carlos would turn up again and she would be unable to say what she had to say in front of him.

Putting the glass down on the worktop, she drew a deep breath and squared her shoulders.

She was going to do this—*now*.

She was barely inside the other room when the sight that met her eyes drove all the breath from her body in a shocked rush. Raul was waiting for her, but it wasn't just the sight of him standing there, big and dark and disturbingly formidable, feet planted firmly on the woven rug before the gas fire, that shook her world. It was the picture frame he held in his hand, head bent, hooded eyes intent on the image in the photograph it held.

And the look on his face twisted her heart in her chest. She knew that look and she knew exactly what it meant. But the real problem was that she knew that what she was about to say could only make things so much worse.

CHAPTER FOUR

THE photograph WAS the first thing that Raul had seen when he walked back into the room. Because with Alannah's instruction in his head that he should sit down he'd been heading for one of the armchairs grouped around the small gas fire, and he was facing that way for the first time, towards the wall and the small round table that stood against it. The table was crammed with photographs, all in frames of different shapes and sizes, some wood, some polished silver, some old, like the picture of her grandmother he recognised from when he had known her before, and some obviously very recent.

It was one of these that had caught his attention.

And what he saw had the power to make him feel as if a brutal knife had just slashed open his heart, letting out all the pain and the loss he had been fighting to hold back ever since he had been dragged away from a business meeting by the worst phone call he had ever received in his life.

'Lorena...Lori...'

The name escaped his lips on a whisper, the pain even of speaking it searing into his soul. His eyes blurred so badly that for a moment he thought—hoped—that he had been wrong and the subject of the photograph was not who he thought it was. But blinking hard as he snatched it up did nothing to help that feeling. In fact it only made it so much worse as it cleared his vision and made it agonisingly plain that he had not been wrong.

Lori's beautiful, delighted face smiled up at him from behind the glass. Her grin was wide, her brown eyes sparkled, her dark hair was tossed by some unseen breeze. She looked totally happy, totally wonderful.

Totally alive.

His hands clenched tight on the picture frame, so tight that he almost felt that the light pine wood would shatter under the pressure of his fingers.

This was wrong—so wrong. Lori was so young. Too young. She was *too* young—had been *too* young. With a terrible lurch of his heart he adjusted the tense of his thoughts as he had had to do so many times in the past twenty-four hours. As he would have to do for the rest of his life—at least until he got used to it.

And he didn't *want* to get used to it. Never!

How could his little sister—his precious, beautiful baby sister, the sister who had been put so carefully into his arms when she was less than a day old and had moved straight into his heart in an instant—be dead while he was still alive? It went against all the laws of nature that he had already had ten years more of life than she would ever know. That at twenty-one her life was already over—finished.

It didn't bear thinking about. He couldn't think about it… His numbed, bruised and battered brain just couldn't take it in.

The photograph was almost invisible behind the burning haze in his eyes. He wanted to lift a hand to brush at them fiercely but somehow his grip wouldn't loosen on the photograph he held. He couldn't let go…

'Raul…'

The voice was low, feminine, gentle…as gentle as the soft fingers that touched his hand, very lightly, very carefully.

'Raul…'

It was an effort to drag his eyes away from the photograph and they wouldn't quite focus when he did. So Alannah's face was still a blur, her expression indistinct when he turned to her.

'What are you doing with a picture of Lori? Why is there a photograph of my sister in your flat?'

'Lori gave it to me.'

Alannah's voice seemed uneven and strangely fuzzy. Or perhaps that was because he was having difficulty concentrating as well as seeing clearly.

'She sent it to me on my birthday.'

Of course. His sister had adored Alannah and she had been overjoyed at the prospect of having her as a sister-in-law. She had been devastated when he had had to tell her that they weren't going to be married after all. In fact telling Lori had been one of the hardest things he had had to do. He had never forgiven Alannah for destroying his sister's dreams along with his own when she had walked out on them.

'You were still in touch with her?'

'Yes.'

There was something wrong with her answer, an edge on the words that he didn't understand, and right now his thinking wasn't clear enough to be able to work out anything like that. He just knew that the way she spoke grated on him, made his skin feel raw as well as his heart.

'Do you know why she was in England? Did she come to see you?'

'Yes.'

There it was again, that ragged, uneven note that twisted something deep inside.

'Raul—' she began but suddenly the dreadful thought that she might not know the full truth pushed him to cut across her words.

'Did you know—Lori—did you know that she…?'

As he drew breath, drew strength to say the hateful word *died—Lori died*—Alannah moved with sudden urgency.

'Oh, don't! Don't!'

Those soft fingers touched his face, covered his mouth to stop, to hold back the dreadful truth. And she was very, very close, the scent of her body surrounding him, the warmth of her skin against his.

'You don't have to,' she whispered. 'I know—at the hospital—I heard…'

'You know?'

The relief was so intense it was almost savage. She knew—and of course she understood. She had been through this tragedy herself so recently. Of all people, she would understand so much. He had someone to share the darkness with.

'I know.'

And this time she leaned even further forward so that her forehead rested against his own. Her breath was warm on his cheek. The soft brush of her hair against his skin was a caress that had him biting his lip against the groan of response that almost escaped him.

From darkness and emptiness his feelings suddenly leapt to burning awareness. Where there had been a sort of suspended animation, the numbness of loss and despair, suddenly a shaft of feeling, sharp and brilliant as a flash of light, delicate and painful as a stiletto, pierced the armour of restraint he had locked round himself and let life back in.

His hand closed around hers where it lay on his arm, strong fingers lacing with her finer, paler ones, and he felt her squeeze his in response to the pressure of his touch. There were no more words, just as there had been no words when he had held her as she cried out her distress in the hospital. He'd envied her those tears then, and he still felt the same way now. His eyes burned but they were dry and gritty. The release that she had found escaped him, though the storm that raged in his heart demanded the expression he couldn't give it.

'Gracias...'

He wasn't quite sure what he was thanking her for. For her understanding, for her touch, for her closeness or just for her silence. The silence that meant he didn't have to try to speak or even to think. Just for this moment he could simply rest as he had been unable to rest since the news had broken. For now, the silence was enough.

But even as he thought that he realised there was something about the silence that was not right. Something that made it not the gentle silence of comfort, of sharing. The silence between two hurting people who had suffered the same terrible loss. Instead Alannah had pulled back—just an inch or so, but she had moved away. And suddenly there was an almost dangerous edge to her stillness. An edge that scraped like sandpaper over his nerves, telling him—warning him that there was something that was wrong here; something that had to be brought into the open.

And instinctively he knew that it had to do with the reason she had brought him up here.

'Alannah…'

His voice sounded rough and husky, as if he hadn't used it in days.

'No…' she said at last, and it was almost a moan, a sound of despair. 'No—don't thank me. Not yet. Not until I've told you everything.'

'Everything?'

Alannah's heart sank right down to somewhere beneath the soles of her feet when she heard the way that Raul's voice had changed, darkened, the deeply suspicious note coming back into it. She wished she could go back just a couple of minutes—retreat to the moment when she had been so close to him. When he had been grateful that she was there.

'What the hell is everything? Just what is it you've

been dancing around telling me? That's obviously the reason you brought me up here and yet you insist on making coffee—doing anything other than tell me!'

'I'm sorry.'

It was barely a whisper. Now that the moment was here her voice threatened to fail her and the fearful race of her heart made the blood pound so loudly inside her head that she could barely hear herself speak.

'I will tell you. I need to explain—about when I met you in the hospital, why I was there—'

'Your brother,' Raul inserted sharply.

'Yes, and—there was more to it than that. Much more. And—oh, I'm *sorry…*'

She had his attention now, dark eyes narrowed, that burning, searching gaze fixed on her face. He must see the glimmer of tears in her eyes, the way she was having to blink them back.

'Sorry for what?' It was low, dangerous, intent. 'Alannah—tell me.'

'I'm sorry…'

Oh, if only she could stop saying that phrase! She felt sure that Raul would pounce on it again like a tiger on its prey. But the fierce scrutiny of his stunning eyes didn't waver, and although his beautiful mouth tightened briefly he didn't say a word. He just waited. And the dark intensity of his silence dried her throat so brutally that she had to fight to force out the words that needed to be said.

'When I said that I knew—about Lori…that I heard in the hospital, that wasn't quite true.'

The mention of his sister's name had stilled him,

focused him totally on one thing. If his gaze had been fierce before then now it burned like a laser.

'And the truth is?'

'That—that—well, I did hear at the hospital, but that was because—it was when I was there for Chris.'

'Your brother?'

Raul was frowning now, clearly having trouble following what she said. And she really couldn't blame him. She was making a terrible mess of this. And it would have been so much better—kinder too—if she had just come out and said it.

'You were at the hospital for your brother…'

'And for Lori…' Somehow she forced it out. 'They were brought in there together.'

Raul's head went back sharply as if reacting to a brutal slap. Confusion, disbelief, suspicion all crossed his face in quick succession and to Alannah's horror it was suspicion that caught and held.

Hard hands clamped around her shoulders, holding her bruisingly tight, and he pushed her away until she was at arm's length so that he could look into her face, probe her eyes.

'But Lori was in a car crash—killed outright. And your brother was ill.'

'No…'

The word was so low and miserable that he must have barely caught it. But he couldn't mistake the way that she shook her head to confirm what she'd said.

'You assumed that—I let you assume that. Because I didn't dare tell you at the time. I was there to tell you. I meant to tell you. But—'

'Tell me *what*?' Raul's voice slashed through her stammering attempt to explain. '*Madre de Dios*, Alannah, tell me what?'

'That Chris and Lori were injured together—in the same crash.' There; it was out. She had actually said it. 'They were in the same car. The crash killed them both.'

This time he was silent so long that for a dreadful moment she thought that, crazily, for some reason he hadn't heard. The fear that she might have to say it all over again was like a twisting pain inside her head and she had just forced herself to open her mouth again to do just that when Raul finally spoke.

'I don't understand. Just what the hell were my sister and your brother doing in any car together? I thought you said she came to see you.'

The hands that held her released their grip with such suddenness that she stumbled backwards, opening up a space between them. But one look into his face stilled her again in an instant.

The dark pools of his eyes above the pallor of his cheeks and the appalling, almost greyish tinge to his skin were alarming. They made Alannah bite her lip hard in distress as she saw him try to take in what she was saying. She knew how much he had doted on his young sister and it tore at her heart to think of what this was doing to him.

'Don't you think you would be more comfortable if we sat down…?'

She couldn't finish the sentence when he suddenly took a couple of steps towards her, rejecting her suggestion with a violent shake of his head, a terrible mixture of anger and pain darkening his eyes.

'I don't want to sit down and I sure as hell don't want to be *comfortable*! I want to know—'

'They were seeing each other,' Alannah blurted out in a rush, desperate to get it said, to get this over with. 'Chris and Lori were a couple. They met one time when she came to see me here and—they were crazy about each other.'

'She never said anything.'

'Of course she didn't. She knew how you'd react. You wouldn't have wanted your sister to date my brother; admit it—you'd have hated it.'

The dangerous expression that flashed across his face told her she was right before a curt nod of Raul's dark head acknowledged the truth of her words.

'I know...' she began but Raul's brutal tones cut across her stumbling words.

'Then you'll know how I feel about the fact that she ever came here to visit you. I told her not to contact you—never to see you again. You broke her heart when you walked out.'

Broke *her* heart, Alannah noted bitterly. Not his— not Raul's. But then she doubted that Raul had a heart to break. At least where she was concerned. His sister Lori had been quite a different matter. And her own heart ached desperately in sympathy for him over that.

'And she was *dating* your brother. If I'd known...'

'You couldn't have stopped her, Raul. She was a grown woman.'

'She was twenty-one!'

'Old enough to know her own mind. And her own heart!'

She had been twenty-one when she'd met him. She'd known her own heart then—known that she wanted to stay with this man for the rest of her life. Until reality had stripped the rose-coloured spectacles from her eyes.

'Her heart…' Raul's scornful laugh dismissed the claim. 'She didn't love him—she couldn't have done.'

'And why not?'

This time Alannah was the one to take a step forward, defiance driving her close to Raul's powerful form in a way that in any other mood she would have avoided at all costs.

'Why couldn't she have loved Chris? Why is that so hard to believe? Or is it just that you don't think that any member of my family is lovable? That because I walked out on you then no Redfern is worth bothering with? Don't take your own bitterness out on—'

'Bitterness!'

Raul's laugh this time was pure cynicism, so harsh it made her flinch back as he tossed it right into her face.

'Don't kid yourself, *querida*! There's no bitterness—that's not what I feel. The truth is that I feel nothing—nothing at all. Except perhaps a trace of relief that you refused my offer of marriage when you did. I dread to think what my life would be like now if you'd accepted—a living hell, I should imagine.'

'Then we've both cause to be grateful it never happened!'

Alannah flung the words at him, putting the bite of conviction into each syllable.

'But you can't blame my behaviour on Chris! He

is—he was,' she amended painfully, faltering as the
black memories hit home, 'a very different person. And
he adored Lori. He would never have hurt her—not…'

Another tidal wave of memory crashed over her
head, killing the words on her tongue, drying her throat
painfully. And the terrible glitter in Raul's dark eyes
told her that he had noticed and even as she began to
feel the fear, to dread what was coming, he pounced
with lethal perception.

'Not?' he echoed viciously. 'Not what, *querida*?
Your brother would never have hurt Lorena, not…?'

He let the sentence trail off, obviously expecting her
to complete it. But Alannah couldn't find the words,
or the strength to use them.

'Tell me.'

It was a tone that had in it all the command, all the arrogance of the generations of aristocrats who had made
up the Marcín dynasty. It was the voice of a man who was
used to being obeyed and expected nothing less right
now. And Alannah felt her legs start to tremble at the
sound of it, her knees threatening to give way beneath her.

'Raul—please…' she tried but he swept the words
aside with a savagely imperious gesture.

'Tell me!' he ordered. 'And tell me the truth—all of
it; I shall know if you lie.'

She'd no doubt about that, Alannah acknowledged
privately. She wouldn't dare to lie to him, fearing the
consequences if she did and he found out. His ability
to read the truth in her face came close to being psychic
and she was afraid of what he would see in her eyes if
she met his. But how could she say…?

'He was driving!'

The words echoed her thoughts so closely that for a dreadful moment she thought she had spoken them out loud. But then to her horror she realised that it was even worse. Raul had seen in her expression the words she couldn't bring herself to say and now he spat them out in savage fury, his eyes pure ice, his expression dark with disgust.

'Your brother was driving the car that crashed, wasn't he? *Wasn't he?*' he demanded again, with brutal emphasis when she flinched away from answering him.

'Yes…'

It was just a whisper, a thin thread of sound. But, hearing it, Raul flung up his arms in a gesture that expressed the violence of his thoughts more than any words could ever manage. Spinning away from her, he paced the width of the living room back and forth, back and forth, making Alannah think fearfully of a caged, ferocious tiger, one that was too big and too powerful to be confined in the small space of her tiny apartment.

'Raul…' she tried but he ignored her, flicking off her trembling use of his name with a brusque shake of his head.

'He wouldn't hurt her,' he muttered, low and dangerous. 'Oh, no, he wouldn't hurt her—wouldn't harm a hair on her head—he just *killed* her!'

CHAPTER FIVE

'CHRIS didn't kill her!'

Alannah struggled to control her voice, to stop if from shaking so much that her words were incomprehensible.

'He wouldn't—'

'Was he drunk?'

'No—it wasn't like that.'

Suddenly aware of the way that she was holding out her hands to Raul, seeming to implore him to listen, Alannah dropped them again hastily, pushing her fingers into the pockets of her jeans to hide the way they shook with nerves.

'Then what was it like?'

At least he had stopped the restless pacing. He had come to a halt but over on the opposite side of the room, well away from her as his molten copper eyes blazed into hers. The physical distance between them might be small in reality, but in Alannah's mind it had suddenly opened up like some huge, un-bridgeable chasm, stretching wide and deep to separate them totally.

'It was an accident—a lorry driver lost control and veered right across, knocking them into the central reservation—no one's fault—just…'

'Just an accident.' Raul's tone put a spin of total disbelief on the words. 'But it wasn't an accident that Lori was here in the first place, was it? That was because you and your brother worked on her. She would never have gone against my wishes…'

'Gone against your wishes!'

Alannah secretly felt that it was relief that he had moved on to another topic, giving her something to attack him with rather than just taking the accusations she couldn't refute, that put a new confidence into her voice, though she wished it didn't sound quite so shrill, so hard and belligerent.

'Do you really think that you had the right to impose *your wishes* on her? That you could interfere in her life and tell her what to do? Dictating to her…'

'I wanted to make sure she never met up with you again. You or any member of your family.'

'And why? Because I wasn't stupid enough to accept your cold-blooded proposal of marriage—does that make me unfit to even associate with any member of your family? I loved Lori.'

'And so you encouraged her to come here and visit—to meet up with your brother—and now because of that she's dead.'

'They're both dead,' Alannah managed flatly, exhaustion draining all the emotion from her voice. 'I lost my brother too.'

'He took my sister with him.'

Raul sounded as if he was choking over the words; as if his throat was closing up around them.

Abruptly he wheeled away from her, his face set and hard as he headed for the door.

'Raul…'

Instinctive concern dragged his name from her lips.

'Where—where are you going?'

'Out.' And don't even think of arguing about it, his savage tone warned.

He couldn't bear to be with her a moment longer. He didn't have to say the actual words, everything about his demeanour, the silent rejection stamped into every rigid line of his body, the proudly held head, said it for him. He was leaving and if she was wise she would let him go.

But that was something Alannah just couldn't do.

She couldn't let him walk out—not like this. Not when he was clearly feeling every bit as wretched as she felt—worse, because he had only just found out the truth about the terrible crash when she at least had had a couple of days to let the bitter reality sink in.

Outside, the night was pitch-black, the rain still pelting down, lashing against the windows. She couldn't bear to think of him being out there, in the darkness, alone, when his mood was already so dark and desolate.

'Oh, no…'

In a flurry of movement she rushed forward, slipped past him so that she reached the door before he did. Whirling round, she flung herself against it, pressing her back hard against the white-painted wood so that he would have to come through her if he truly wanted to get out.

And he was quite capable of doing that, the look on his face, the burning glare he flung her told her without any need for words. Never before had he seemed so big, so strong, so totally overwhelming so that her stomach clenched into tight knots of near panic, her throat drying painfully.

'Alannah…move.' Raul's voice was a low, savage snarl of warning, his tone threatening terrible repercussions if she didn't do as he commanded. 'Don't even think of trying to stop me.'

The ferocity of his expression, the danger in his tone kept her mute, but somehow she forced herself to set her mouth tight, lift her chin, as she shook her head in silent defiance, even though her knees were threatening to buckle beneath her as her eyes met the icy blaze of his.

'Get out of my way…'

'I won't—I can't!'

That 'can't', or something of the desperation in her tone, got through to him, making him still suddenly, his head going back, molten eyes narrowing to sharply assessing slits. That terrible grey tinge to his skin was back and it was that that told her she was right to do this—whatever it took. However he reacted. He was a danger to himself in this state, although, being Raul, he would deny it furiously if she said anything.

'Can't?' he questioned harshly. 'What the hell—?'

'I *can't* let you go—not like this. I can't see you walk out into a city you don't know—on a night like this…'

A curtain of tears was blurring her vision but she could still see the way that his stance changed, becoming slightly less aggressive, less antagonistic. His silence was more eloquent than any words could ever be.

'You'd care?' he said at last, his voice cracking on the last word.

'Of course I'd care.'

'I'm a big boy, Alannah. I can take care of myself.'

'I don't care how big and ugly you are—I'm not letting you go. You've had a shock…' Carefully she lowered her voice, pitched on a softer note. 'You're not thinking straight…'

Her tone was gentle, Raul registered. As gentle as it had been when she had come to him earlier; when she had reached out to him from the darkness. And just as it had then, her gentleness touched some needy spot in his mind so that for the first time in a terrible twenty-four hours he was still. Totally still. Even his whirling, raging, aching thoughts seemed to have stopped.

In the silence he watched her ease herself away from the door and come towards him. Once again he felt the softness of her touch on his hand.

'Stay until Carlos comes,' she said and still in silence he nodded slowly.

Once again the silence was enough.

'Thank you,' she said, in much the same way that he had said *'Gracias'* to her a short time before, so that he knew without having to be told just how she too was grateful to have someone sharing the darkness with her.

It was then that he caught the faint waft of some perfume, soft and subtly leafy, that came from the shampoo she had used on her hair. But underneath it was another scent, richer, warmer, more sensual, intimate. More womanly. It was the scent of Alannah herself. The scent of her body, her skin and her hair, and it hit straight to his starved senses like a blow, melting the numbness in his head so fast that he reeled under the impact of the rush of blood through his veins. The throb of hunger was so powerful, so primitive that it forced all other thoughts from his mind.

'Thank you,' Alannah said again and the hand that touched his moved very slightly, her thumb stroking over his skin.

'De nada.'

Her kiss was unexpected. It was light, soft, delicate. Just a press of her lips against the side of his cheek, nothing passionate or sensual in it. There, and then gone again. But the feelings it sparked off were far from gentle, far from light.

They were hot and needy and yearning for more.

After the storm of anger, of rejection and blind fury—fury at her brother, the driver of the lorry she had talked of, at fate—there was another storm building inside him now. One of heat and fire—and a hunger he couldn't stamp down. From feeling dead, lost, empty he began to be warm, vital, alive, sensation and need stinging along every nerve path, bringing his senses startlingly, explosively awake.

He felt sure she must sense it, feel it in the tension in his body, hear it in the changed pattern of his breathing.

'Alannah…'

His use of her name was thick, rough, his voice raw

and thickened by the sensual fire that flared within him. He suddenly found that he had had enough of stillness, of silence. He wanted to assert light in the face of darkness, heat in the face of cold…

Life in the face of death.

Turning his head, he caught her lips with his, snatching his hands free to clamp them at the back of her skull, fingers threading through the softness of her hair, twisting to hold her just where he wanted her as he took her mouth with all the ferocity of the need he couldn't control. His blood throbbed at his temples and heat pounded between his legs, making him so hard so fast that it was almost painful. And as Alannah's mouth opened under his he felt the red haze of desire flood his mind, driving away the memories he couldn't bear to remember.

This was what he wanted—to forget—to stop himself from thinking—to lose himself in fierce, mindless response—in fierce, mindless sex. And this woman had always been able to make him forget about anything but her.

To make him think only of her and the wild, blazing fires they built between them.

'Alannah…' he said again but this time her name was a whisper of seduction against her lips as he drew her breath into his own lungs. 'Alannah, *querida*…'

Alannah, *querida*… The words seemed to swirl around inside Alannah's head, taking her thoughts with them as sensation after sensation fizzed through every cell in her body, obliterating logic or control, and only leaving awareness and need.

She should have known that it was a mistake to come close to Raul like this. Should have known that her own memories, her weakness where he was concerned, the sensual burn that he seemed to be able to awaken in her simply by existing, would only risk putting her into his power if she broke through the careful invisible barriers she had tried to put between them ever since the moment she had first seen him in the hospital room. She had weakened then and all but thrown herself into his arms, but the storm of weeping that had overtaken her had driven every other thought from her head.

Her only need then had been of comfort and support. It was when she had recovered a little, when she had calmed enough to draw breath, that she became aware of other feelings, sensations she had thought long since dead and now was forced to realise were only buried, just below the surface, waiting only for a touch, a kiss to break through her defences and leave her aching for more.

She'd known she was in danger when she'd felt that sense of loss as Raul had walked away from her in the kitchen when she had been so sure that he was about to kiss her. Loss and disappointment were the feelings of someone who was still tied to this man in spite of all the time they had spent apart, and her determination to put him out of her mind, out of her heart. She didn't want to be tied to him in any way. She didn't love him—how could she love a man who had only ever seen her as a body, a brood mare on which to breed the heirs he and his family longed for?

But you didn't have to love to want—to hunger for a touch, a kiss, to overreact when he gave her one and feel a sense of loss when he denied her the other.

She had vowed to keep her distance. To keep a grip on herself and the feelings she seemed unable to erase along with the love she had once felt for him. And she would have done so. She would have managed that if she hadn't come out here and seen Raul with the picture frame in his hands, the terrible look of loss and sorrow draining all the colour from his face as he stared down at the photograph of his young sister. The sister he had so recently learned was dead, just like her own brother.

And she wouldn't have been human if she hadn't felt for him and needed to go to him to offer compassion and sympathy, to help him in the same way that he had helped her as he'd held her and let her sob out her grief against the strength of his chest, with his powerful arms closed about her.

That was what he'd done for her—and what she had planned to do for him. But she didn't have the strength that Raul possessed, the self-control—the indifference—that had kept him firmly distant from her even as he held her close. She had only to touch him and she was lost in a world of sensation where common sense and self-preservation had no place. From the moment she had felt the heat of his skin underneath her fingertips, she had wanted more. The scent of his body was so familiar and yet so alien, clean and faintly musky, touched with a tang of something citrus: intensely personal, intensely masculine—intensely Raul.

The fierce rage that had gripped him when he'd

learned the truth had clouded that feeling. Clouded but not destroyed it. And moving close again now had been all that it had taken to reawaken it.

She'd told herself that the kiss was simply one of comfort, a gesture of sympathy, but somewhere deep in her soul she'd known that she was only denying the truth even to herself. And the truth was that she might try to fight against him, against the sensual tug of his physical appeal, the way his body seemed to call to hers, but she couldn't fight herself. That kiss might have started out as a kiss of compassion, but in the instant that her lips had touched his skin, feeling its warmth and tasting the slightly salt flavour of it against her tongue, she had known that she was lost.

Every moment of loss, of longing, of need that she had ever known, ever felt with this man came flooding back into her mind, sweeping away rational thought with the ferocity and speed of a tidal wave and leaving nothing in its place but the whirling, surging wild waters of desire.

The last thing she heard was that raw, hungry muttering of her own name as his head turned, his mouth taking hers. But from that moment the world and everything else in it faded into the red, swirling haze that was all that was in her mind. Her eyes closed as his mouth took hers, his kiss crushing her lips apart, breath mingling, tongues tangling together. Such was the force of his kiss that she swayed violently and would have fallen if the steely strength of his arms hadn't come round her, fastening tight and holding her up, clamped hard against the lean power of his body.

'R-Raul…' She choked his name in a sound of need, of pleading, huskily hungry—and the only word she could think of; the only thought in her head.

She felt his smile against her mouth. His hands were hard against her back. Big hands, hot hands, heavy hands, fingers splayed out along her spine, burning her skin through the protection of her T-shirt, holding her where he wanted her as he took another kiss and then one more.

'You're beautiful,' he muttered against her cheek. 'Beautiful.'

Those stroking hands were never still, always moving, always tracing hot erotic patterns over her back, sliding under her T-shirt at her waist, briefly searing over her skin so that she couldn't hold back a murmur of response as she arched into the caress like a cat responding to a sensual stroke. His mouth was a teasing torment, his tongue like silk against her lips. The thunder in her blood was drowning out all her ability to think.

She wanted…longed…yearned…

She needed more.

She had always wanted more. It had been Raul who had held back; Raul who had said that they should wait. Proud Spanish aristocrat that he was, he had wanted her to come to his bed untouched. He had wanted to know that he was the only man in her life, that only a virgin bride would be the mother of his child.

And that memory was bitter enough to slice through the heated haze that flooded her mind.

'No…'

Somehow she managed to make her tongue frame the single syllable. Somehow she managed to force her treacherous body to pull back, away from him, away from his kisses, away from his touch. The few steps she managed took her up against one of the armchairs so that she was forced to stop, not quite as far away from him as she had wanted.

'No…' She tried again but with little more conviction than the first time. Every one of her senses cried out in harsh protest at the cruel restraint she forced on them. Every awoken nerve demanded the satisfaction she was denying it.

'No?'

Raul's echoing of the single word had so much more behind it that it made her flinch to hear it. There was an open scepticism that questioned her denial, a note of incredulity that made it plain he didn't believe her, and underneath it all there was the rough thread of dark desire—a desire she had thwarted by drawing away. And the terrible thing was that that desire, dark and disturbing and oh, so dangerous, was what was running through her veins, making her shudder inwardly in response to its burning demand.

But she wouldn't give in to it. Couldn't give in to it.

'This isn't going to happen. This isn't what I want.'

'Isn't what you want?' His voice lashed at her, filled with a brutal cynicism. 'Forgive me if I don't believe you. I don't think you know what you want.'

'Oh, but I do!' Alannah shook her head violently then stopped abruptly as she realised that she was contradicting her words with the foolish gesture. 'I do.'

'Then what?' he snarled viciously, the burn of frustration still there in his voice. 'What the hell do you want?'

'I want—I want…'

Desperately she snatched at the only thing that came to mind. The memory of what they had been talking about. The reason why she had brought him here in the first place.

'I want you to forgive my brother. I want you to acknowledge that he and Lorena loved each other and—and…'

Near-panic had got her this far, the rush of need to say something, anything driving the words out before she had a chance to think. But now, seeing his face, seeing the way that cold fury had turned his eyes opaque, the white marks of rage etched around his nose and mouth, she felt herself falter, felt the words elude her.

'And…' Raul prompted icily when she hesitated.

'And I—we—we'd like to bury them together. We'd like you to give us permission to bury Chris and Lorena in the same grave so that they—they could be…'

Together.

The word sounded inside her head but she totally lacked the strength to say it. She couldn't have managed another word if her life depended on it. And in the silence that followed she felt as if a window must have blown open in the force of the wind outside, letting in the cold and the wet so that she shivered in the sudden chill of the air as if the temperature had actually dropped to zero around her.

'You want me to forgive your brother…'

Raul's tone was so calm, so unemotional that

Alannah blinked in confusion to hear it. Was it possible—was he actually going to be reasonable about this? She could read nothing in his shuttered face, his hooded eyes hiding every last trace of what he was feeling from her.

'And you want me to leave my sister here…and you think that coming on to me is the way to soften me up to give you what you want?'

'Coming on?' Alannah gasped in shocked disbelief. 'But I didn't—I wasn't! How could you think that?'

The sound of a loud buzzing noise intruded into her stunned protest, making her start in shock and stare round dazedly, looking for the source of the sound.

Raul, however, reacted immediately, pulling one hand free and snatching his mobile phone from his jacket pocket. Sitting on one arm of the settee, he thumbed it on and spoke sharply into it.

'*Sí?* Carlos…'

Carlos. Of course.

Alannah tensed sharply as she realised just who was at the other end of the phone. A swift glance at the clock on the wall confirmed her suspicions. The thirty minutes Raul had stipulated were up—just—and almost exactly to the second his driver had arrived to collect him as he had been instructed.

So would Raul leave now, as he had originally planned? Her heart lurched sickeningly at the thought, the tension in her body growing worse. Did she want him to go or to stay? She had no way she could answer that, even to herself.

'*Momento…*' Raul said into the phone, then, still

holding it to his ear, he glanced across into Alannah's outraged face. For a moment he simply watched her consideringly, eyes narrowed in cold assessment, and with a curt, sharp nod of dark satisfaction he turned his attention back to the phone.

'Yes,' he said sharply, using English deliberately, she was sure, so that she had no option but to understand what he was saying. 'Yes, I'm done here—more than ready to leave. I'll be down in a minute.'

He was going. He was leaving, and nothing was going to stop him; his tone, his expression, the cold gleam in his eyes made that only too plain. He was leaving and… That was as far as she got. She didn't have time even to finish the thought before Raul snapped off his phone and, still with his eyes fixed on her face, dropped it back in the direction of his jacket pocket. Then slowly, silently, holding her wide-eyed gaze with his own, he stood up and smoothed down his trousers, brushed a speck of something—a purely imaginary speck of something, Alannah was sure—from the front of his jacket.

'My chauffeur is waiting,' he said and Alannah actually gasped out loud because it was as if the ice in his voice had been physically real, hitting her brutally in the face as he spoke. 'And it's more than time I left.'

'But…' Alannah tried, knowing she couldn't let him go without an answer, though in her heart she knew what it was going to be, something that was confirmed by the look that flashed from those dark golden eyes.

'The answer is no, Miss Redfern…'

She recoiled sharply, flinching away from the stiff formality of his use of her name.

'There is no way that I will leave my sister here to be buried alongside the man who killed her.'

'But he didn't…' Alannah tried again but Raul ignored her interjection, talking over it as if it had never happened.

'My family and yours should never have had any contact—we should have stayed at the opposite ends of the earth.'

'Why? Because my ordinary family just aren't good enough to mix with the likes of the high and mighty Marquez Marcín dynasty?'

Alannah no longer cared what she was saying or how she sounded. She only wanted to lash out, hurt him as she was hurting. Make him bleed as she felt that she was bleeding to death inside. She no longer knew or cared if it was for herself or her brother—or for poor little Lorena that her heart was breaking. Only that she had to scream out the agony or break down completely.

'Well, let me tell you that I wish to God we'd never met. That it was the worst thing that ever happened to me—the worst day of my life—when you walked into it.'

If she thought that by lashing out she'd get through to him, make him react, then she was bitterly disappointed. Where she'd expected anger there was simply coldness, where she would have thought there would be emotion there was a frozen stillness, a terrible quiet in which he looked down his long, straight nose at her, his mouth twisting in vicious contempt.

'Then the feeling is entirely mutual,' he tossed at her. 'I can assure you that I feel exactly the same. I wish to hell that I had never met you—never set eyes on you…'

'Never...'

Twice Alannah tried to add to the single word. But both times she opened her mouth and had to close it again hastily because nothing came out. Raul just watched her, hands clenched into fists and pressed tight against his narrow hips.

'Wished you'd never met me,' she finally got out. 'Then why would you have wanted to marry me?'

Oh, why couldn't she stop? Why did she have to keep stabbing at him, pushing him to come back at her with something even worse?

Which of course he did.

'You know why. I needed an heir.'

Well, she'd always known that. She'd just never expected him to come right out and say it so bluntly.

She'd hesitated a moment too long and those sharp golden eyes had caught the faint flicker of unease in her face, the way she had recoiled from his words.

'Oh, come on, Alannah,' he mocked cruelly. 'You surely didn't think I was going to say that I loved you? You can't have wanted that?'

This time she had no trouble finding the words, or the strength of voice to throw them at him.

'You're damn right I wouldn't! I wouldn't have wanted any such thing from you—it would disgust me—repel me—and besides, I doubt very much that you know what love is. It's certainly not a feeling that you've ever experienced for any woman, even one you once asked to marry you.'

'I'd have to agree with you there.' Raul drew himself up and inclined his head in a cold, controlled acknowledgement of her accusation. 'Love is a very unreliable foundation on which to base one's choice of bride.'

'No, you put more emphasis on the fact that no other man has ever slept with her than any such untrustworthy feelings.'

'Well, that didn't last long, did it?' Raul mocked. 'As soon as I asked to marry you, you realised that you weren't made for monogamy and set out to make up for what you'd been missing.'

'But the one thing I didn't miss was you!'

With her head defiantly high in the air, she stalked past him and out into the tiny hallway, flinging open the door with a wild gesture that had it banging into the opposite wall.

'And now I'd prefer it if you left. Your chauffeur is waiting and you wouldn't want to keep him hanging around. And this time I'd be grateful if you stayed away—for good.'

'Don't worry.'

Raul headed for the door with an alacrity that would have been positively insulting if she had had enough left in her heart to feel a further insult.

'I'm not likely to want to come back. It'll be a cold day in hell before I ever want to see you or any member of your family ever again.'

'Well, that suits me,' Alannah tossed after him as he strode out the door. 'Believe me, if I was forced to see you again then I'd know that I was very definitely in that hell you mentioned.'

She slammed the door shut after his retreating form, hearing the sound echo throughout her flat as she sank

back against the wall, her whole body shaking with the
after-effects of the emotional storm that had had her
in its grip.

CHAPTER SIX

RAUL tossed the last of his clothing into the case that lay open on the bed and then brought the lid down on it with a bang. Fastening the zip with a rough, wrenching movement, he pulled it off the bed, carried it through into the adjoining sitting room and deposited it beside the door, ready for the hotel porter to come and collect it. Another hour, and he would be out of here.

And it couldn't happen soon enough. He'd known from the start that this trip to England was going to be hell on earth, but the truth was that he had never imagined how hellish it could be. Accepting the appalling news of Lori's death, getting through the formalities and arranging for her funeral had been terrible enough. But then there had been the added twist of torture that had come in the meeting with Alannah, the discovery that it had been her brother who had…

'No…'

He aimed a vicious kick at the side of the suitcase as his mind shied away from thinking of the crash that had killed his sister. The passage of four days since the news had broken had done nothing to blunt the sharply jagged edges of that pain and the news he had received just that afternoon had only stirred up all the sorrow even more.

Rubbing the palms of his hands fiercely across his face, over his aching, burning eyes, Raul could only wish that he could wipe away the memory of the past few days as he did so. He had thought that it couldn't get any worse, but fate had had one last little trick in store, one further twist of the knife that made the loss of his sister even more unbearable to think of.

But if he didn't think of Lorena then there was only one path his thoughts went down and that was one that was no more comfortable than the first.

The image of Alannah Redfern's lissom body, her stunning face and the clear, emerald-green of those almond-shaped eyes was always ready to slide into his mind if he let his guard down. It was there in his memory during the day, distracting him from work, heating his blood and making him hard and hungry in the space of one heavy beat of his heart.

He could still feel the brutal kick of disgust that had landed on his senses with the realisation of just why she had kissed him, why she had responded to him so eagerly, so—for a moment at least, he had actually believed—sweetly. Disillusionment had set in fast and the rage that had replaced it had been coldly savage. If he had thought that he hated her before, then it had been nothing to the way he felt now. He had had to get out of her flat before his rage had got the better of him. And since then his fury had been directed at himself and the way that he couldn't forget.

At night the same images of her kept him from sleep, and when he did eventually doze off then the vision of her softly yielding naked body opening under his turned his dreams into burningly erotic fantasies, so real that he could have sworn that she was actually there. Waking in the dark to tangled sheets, with his own skin slick with sweat, the memory of the taste of her mouth still on his tongue, the scent of her flesh in his nostrils was a sensual torment that had him pacing the floor in the middle of the night, or raiding the mini-bar for something strong enough to give him a chance at sleep.

It never worked and after two long, wakeful nights and two cold, sorrow-filled days he felt like a bad-tempered dog, snarling inwardly and ready to bite.

The final straw had been when he had discovered that his mobile phone was missing. He hadn't even noticed that it was not in his possession until his father had contacted him in his hotel room, desperate to know what was going on. Since then he had turned the room upside down, emptied every drawer, checked in every pocket and still not found it. It was only as he was packing to return home that he had realised where it must be.

He had had the phone in his hand in Alannah's flat. He'd spoken to Carlos, saying he would be down in a moment and…

A string of savage expletives escaped his lips and he raked his hands viciously through his hair as he remembered switching off the phone and dropping it—he thought—back into his jacket pocket. He had been concentrating so hard on reining in his temper that he must have must have missed the pocket and let it fall, unnoticed, onto the cushions of the chair where he'd been sitting. And he had walked out of her flat in such a fury that he hadn't noticed that he'd left it. He could almost picture it now, down in the crack between the cushions, silent and unseen.

Damn it to hell, he would have to send Carlos round to pick it up.

He was heading for the phone on the desk when the knock came at the door. The porter, come for his bag.

'Momento!'

Checking in his pocket that he had cash for a tip, he strode to the door, opened it and stared in blank bemusement at the person outside.

The person who had just filled his thoughts with unwanted sensual memories.

The person he had tried so damned hard to forget and failed so miserably at it.

'Alannah!'

It was as if he had summoned her up. As if simply by thinking of her he had somehow brought her here, to stand in the corridor. As if she had walked out of his dreams and into reality.

And the reality was much better than the dream.

Her hair was loose and tumbled softly about her face, the pale skin was totally untouched by make-up except for some mascara that darkened her fine lashes and a slick of gloss over her lips that made her look as if she had just run her tongue along them, moistening them slightly. She was dressed in a soft pale green dress, one with a skirt that swirled around her slender calves, with the innumerable small buttons fastening the front. It made his mouth dry just to see them. When the thought of the sensual delight of setting himself to opening each and every one of those pearly discs slid into his head he clamped down on it hard, fighting against the risk of it reducing him to the state of some tongue-tied adolescent whose raging hormones could not be brought under control.

'I brought you this…'

Her tone was stiff and her eyes didn't quite meet his, their mossy-green gaze focused somewhere over his shoulder as if she was looking at someone else there. She lifted her hand, holding it out flat. In the centre of her palm lay the missing mobile phone.

'You left it in my flat.'

'*Gracias.*'

His own voice was rough and husky, as if it had come from a very sore throat, and even in his own ears it sounded brusque and dismissive. The small movement had stirred the air, bringing the scent of her body to him, and the combination of clean, feminine skin combined with a delicate, softly floral scent assailed his senses like a physical attack. He almost snatched the phone from her, knowing that the feel of her hand, the warmth of her flesh against his fingertips would be like setting a match to paper-dry tinder, threatening to send him up in flames in a heartbeat.

'I found it down the side of the chair. You must have dropped it there when…'

A wash of colour flooded up into her cheeks as her voice trailed off and he knew that like him she was remembering just why the phone had been left on the chair in the first place.

'I was wondering where it was.'

Was it only in his own ears or did he really sound so appallingly stiff and stilted? He didn't seem to be able to make his mouth work normally. It was as if his tongue had suddenly become stiff and swollen in his mouth.

Or perhaps it was because of the way that his eyes were fixed on the soft, peachy fullness of her mouth. Remembering the feel of it against his, the taste of her on his lips. The way that she had kissed him and the heated response of her body. The heated, deliberately calculated response.

'I'd just decided that it must be in your flat and I was about to send Carlos round to fetch it.'

'Well, now you have it back.'

Alannah's response was low and strangely flat. She was back to being the washed-out creature he had first seen in the hospital room on the day he had arrived in England. There was little trace of the seductive siren he had kissed; even less of the hissing, spitting vixen who had thrown him out of her flat in no uncertain terms. He was shocked to find that it was the vixen he missed most.

Raul's conscience gave an uncomfortable twist so that he could almost hear his late mother demanding just where were his manners? Hadn't she taught him better than this? It was ridiculous having this stiff-voiced conversation with him in the open doorway and her standing outside in the corridor. Even though this was a private suite, at any moment someone could come past—a member of the hotel staff, the porter coming for his case.

He stepped back, holding the door wider open.

'I'm sorry—won't you come in?'

The look she gave him was another reproof to his conscience. And the brief flash of her green eyes only made her face look even more pale and drawn, emphasising the shadows under her eyes.

'You look as if you're about to drop. Come in and sit down for a moment.'

'I don't think…'

He thought that he was being perfectly polite, that he had even added a touch of concern, but from the expression on her face he might just as well have suggested that he slit her throat right here and now. He felt his jaw tighten, his mouth compressing.

'I am capable of being perfectly civilized…'

When she still hesitated, he gave up, flinging up his hands in exasperation and striding back into the room, leaving the door open behind him. Let her make her own decision.

'Thank you.'

To his amazement she had actually followed him, stepping over the threshold of the door like a wary cat moving into alien territory. And, watching her, he knew that he had lied.

He might have said that he was capable of being civilised; he would even have been prepared to swear to it if necessary. But civilised was not what this woman made him feel. Just the soft sound of her voice made his pulse leap with thoughts of a huge bed, soft pillows, clean sheets and Alannah, warm and welcoming, beside him. The scent of her skin made hunger clutch, hard and hot, low down in his body, so that, turning again, to see her behind him, it was all that he could do to force his mouth into some sort of a smile.

'I'll get Carlos to take you back. It's the least I can do—to say thank you. Why don't you sit down?'

He waved a hand towards the big leather-covered settee that stood in the middle of the large sitting room and Alannah's eyes followed the gesture but she silently shook her head and stayed right where she was.

'Isn't this the point at which I should offer you a coffee?' he asked and to his surprise saw the stiffness of her face suddenly crumble and a real, genuine smile broke through the careful restraint she'd imposed.

'If you did, do you think that we'd get to drink it? We don't seem to have had much luck so far.'

Did she know what it did to him to see her eyes light up like that, if only for a moment? To see that lush mouth curve in warmth in a way that it so seldom did when he was around? He might tell himself that he hated this woman—detested the way she'd treated him, and now loathed her entire family for the destruction her brother had wreaked on his—but the truth was much more complicated. He just couldn't get her out of his mind. He was addicted to her and the way he had been feeling the past couple of days was comparable to withdrawal symptoms.

He had needed his 'fix' of Alannah and his symptoms had started to subside as soon as she had appeared at his door. He knew what would really cure him of

GET FREE BOOKS and a FREE MYSTERY GIFT WHEN YOU PLAY THE...

Just scratch off the silver box with a coin. Then check below to see the gifts you get!

SLOT MACHINE GAME!

YES! I have scratched off the silver box. Please send me the 4 FREE books and mystery gift for which I qualify. I understand I am under no obligation to purchase any books, as explained on the back of this card. I am over 18 years of age.

P8CI

Mrs/Miss/Ms/Mr _____ Initials _____

BLOCK CAPITALS PLEASE

Surname _____

Address _____

_____

Postcode _____

7	7	7	**Worth FOUR FREE BOOKS plus a BONUS Mystery Gift!**
🍒	🍒	🍒	**Worth FOUR FREE BOOKS!**
♣	♣	♣	**Worth ONE FREE BOOK!**
🔔	🔔	🔔	**TRY AGAIN!**

Visit us online at www.millsandboon.co.uk

THE READER SERVICE™
FREE BOOK OFFER
FREEPOST CN81
CROYDON
CR9 3WZ

NO STAMP
NECESSARY
IF POSTED IN
THE U.K. OR N.I.

If offer card is missing write to: The Reader Service, PO Box 676, Richmond, TW9 1WU

them and that was to give in to the demands his addicted body was making that he took her in his arms, kissed her—took her to bed.

Or would that only make the sexual craving so much worse for having given in to it and actually experiencing, rather than imagining, the pleasure he knew was just waiting for him in her gorgeous body?

'OK, no coffee.'

But she wasn't looking at him any more. Her attention had been caught by the sight of the packed suitcase standing beside the now closed door and she was staring at it as if it held some special fascination for her.

'You're leaving.'

'In about an hour.'

Alannah didn't know how she felt about that. She was shocked and confused by the sudden stab of pain that shot through her at the sight of the case. Was it the thought of him leaving that brought such distress? That if she hadn't come here today, just now, then she would have missed him? He would have packed and left— and she would never have known. Did she really care?

Oh, who was she kidding? She cared. She had always cared. She might have tried to stop loving him, had spent two long years praying that the feelings would go away, but all he had to do was to walk back into her life and she was lost all over again. Wasn't that why she was here, now, when she had told herself— told him—that she never wanted to see him again?

Oh, yes, so much that she had jumped at the chance that having to return his damn phone to him would bring. Raul, on the other hand, had been 'about to send

Carlos round to fetch it'. Just as he was going to get Carlos to drive her back home. It had been the phone he had wanted; not any chance to see her again. Instead, he had packed and was on his way, going back to Spain, going out of her life, without a word. If she had any sense, she would get out of here now.

If she had really had any sense then she wouldn't even have come into the room at his invitation.

She didn't really know quite why she had accepted that invitation. She'd known that walking into the room was like walking into the lion's den—almost putting her head into the beast's jaws and asking him to bite it off. But there had been something in his face that had made it impossible to do what was sensible. He'd looked tired, lost, lonely—strangely vulnerable. She'd known she should just turn and walk away but she just couldn't do it.

But now she was forced to wonder if she had just been imagining things. Had she only seen in his face what she had wanted to see and deceived herself to what was really there?

'There's nothing to stay for now. Everything's been done…'

Alannah was thankful that Raul's attention was on his phone. He'd switched it on and was checking the missed-calls register, so he didn't see the way her face changed in reaction to that dismissive 'nothing to stay for'. She had a welcome moment to catch herself up, push the foolish weakness aside, and even managed to inject some much needed lightness into her tone when she asked, 'Have you missed anything important?'

'Most from my father.' Raul was still scrolling through the numbers. 'He wants minute-by-minute reports of everything.'

'It must be very hard for him.'

Alannah's voice was low as she thought of the desperate state her mother was in, unable to believe that her beloved son was gone for good. She hadn't eaten a thing since the accident and only that morning Helena had declared that she had nothing to live for, that she could see no reason to go on.

'He's lost his daughter.'

'He's lost more than that.'

Something had put a new harshness into Raul's voice and his sudden stillness alerted her to the fact that he had stopped messing with his phone and his dark head had lifted, bronze eyes looking straight at her.

Cold bronze eyes looking straight at her.

'What is it?'

'You don't know?' The way he said it made it clear that he believed she was just pretending.

'Know what?'

She had to have been fooling herself when she'd thought that he was looking vulnerable—had she actually used the word *lost*? There was nothing in the least bit lost about him now and his face was set in such harsh lines that there was no way at all she could spot any chink in his personal armour. He was angry, he was cold, he was totally closed off against her and she had no idea why. The man who had invited her in, the man she had glimpsed so briefly when he had actually joked about making her coffee, had disappeared completely and it was because she had seen him, even for such a short time, that she felt the loss like some brutal slash across her heart. Just for a moment she had seen the other Raul, the man she had thought he was. The man she had given her heart to, and now he was gone.

But had he ever truly existed? Was that man just a figment of her imagination and this one, this cold-eyed, bitter-mouthed, icily angry monster before her the real Raul? The one he had never let her see until it was too late.

'Tell me,' she said when he simply glared at her without speaking. 'Raul, tell—'

'So you're claiming you didn't know? That there was something your precious brother didn't tell you? Some secret he didn't share?'

'There must have been or I wouldn't be asking now. Raul—what are you talking about?'

'The baby.'

The words came at her like bullets fired from a gun, hard and fast and meant to be lethal, as Raul slammed the phone down on the table without a care for any damage he might do to it.

'Did you know about the baby?'

'What baby? Whose baby? Are you saying…?'

She broke off sharply as realisation dawned, her hand going to her mouth in shock. Raul's savage silent nod seemed to confirm her fears but still she had to say the words to make sure they were the truth.

'Lo—Lori was pregnant?'

Again came that curt, cold nod that was somehow far more terrifying than if he had lost his temper and raged at her. The fearful control he was imposing on himself to remain so silent, so still after that one violent gesture with the phone spoke more eloquently of the way he was feeling than any words could possibly do.

'But how…?'

A savage, burning glare from those molten eyes told her just how stupid he thought that question. And that was something she didn't need telling. Of course she hadn't needed to ask. There was only one person who could have fathered Lorena's baby.

'Chris… How far gone was she?'

'Almost two months, they said.'

'I didn't know.'

Once more those dark eyes flashed in her direction, warning her that he didn't believe her.

'I *didn't* know!'

There was a long, terrible silence. A silence that tugged and twisted painfully on Alannah's nerves, and then at last, just when she had given up all hope of it, Raul slowly nodded.

'No, I don't think you did. You would have told me if you knew when—when you told me all the rest.'

'Yes, I would.' Alannah's tone was soft. 'And if it helps any, I think she was planning on telling you— or at least her father—very soon. They said they had a secret but that I'd have to wait to find out.'

She'd thought it was that they were going to get engaged. But perhaps they had planned on that too. The tears burned like acid at the backs of her eyes but surprisingly none of them fell. For the first time in days she felt as if she was all cried out, no tears possible to moisten her dry, aching eyes.

'Though I suspect that my mother knew.'

Only now, looking back, did she see this as some further explanation of just why her mother had reacted so very badly to the news of Chris's death. Now, at last, she understood the way that Helena had kept muttering about the way that her future had been taken from her as well as her son. At the time it had only made partial sense.

'That would explain why she's so very desolate about this. If she's lost not just my brother but her dream of a grandchild too then it's no wonder she's so desperately low. Nothing seems to even get through to her. Which would be understandable if they told her before they left.'

'While I have still to tell my father. I have to tell him how when your brother died he not only took my father's daughter, my sister, with him but he also took the one thing my father wanted most in all the world: a grandchild to hold in his arms.'

The roughness of his voice told her just how hard he was going to find it.

On an impulse she headed for the mini-bar, found a small bottle of the cognac Raul favoured and tipped half of it into a glass. Without a word she held it out to Raul and watched as he tossed it back. The way that the lean bronze lines of his throat tightened as he swallowed made a small kick of response jerk in her stomach.

'*Gracias.*'

Understanding was what had made her react in this

way, and understanding was what kept her close. She knew what he was going through, having endured it herself. She knew what had put the shadows under his eyes, the grey tinge on his skin. And she knew how he must be dreading telling his father. Matias Marquez Marcín had come late to fatherhood. He had been forty when his son was born, ten years older when his second child, his daughter, Lorena, had come into the world. His health had taken a battering in the past few years and this latest sorrow must have hit him hard.

'Is your father still unwell?'

Raul nodded slowly, the shadows in his eyes and his sombre expression revealing more than his deliberately controlled response.

'He had another stroke just before Christmas. He looks so fragile that I fear a puff of wind would blow him away.'

'There will be other grandchildren.'

'Mine?'

The single word was raw with bitterness and the golden eyes burned with unspoken accusation. He didn't say that the grandchildren he had hoped to give his father would have been the ones he'd planned on having with her, the only reason he had asked her to marry him, but he didn't need to actually speak the words. They were there, in the atmosphere, like letters shaped in ice that came between them with their bitter memories of the past.

'I doubt if I'll marry—I suggested it once and decided it was not for me. I'll not put my head in that noose again.'

The dark, sidelong glance he shot her told her that like her he was thinking of the marriage that had never been between them. Not for the first time she sent up a little prayer of thankfulness that she had never let him see that she knew the real reasons he had ever proposed to her.

'My father knew that if he was to hope for heirs then he had to look to my sister. At least if he was to have grandchildren while he still had the strength to hold them. Even if I created children—would they come in time?'

'I'll pray they do.'

Without thinking she reached out a hand, rested it on Raul's powerful forearm where the way that he had rolled up his shirtsleeve exposed the tanned skin, lightly dusted with black hair. His skin was warm and smooth under her touch and the feel of hard bone and muscle sent a sensation like an electrical shock running up from her fingertips and along every tingling nerve.

She saw him stiffen slightly, saw his dark eyes flick down to where her fingers rested on his arm and then back up to her face.

'Alannah…' he said, just once, soft and low, and he placed the cognac glass down on the table beside him without ever taking his gaze from hers.

A sudden stillness seemed to freeze the air, paralysing her lungs so that her breathing seemed to stop, she even felt her heartbeat slow to a barely there thread of a pulse. It was as if the rest of the world had dissolved into a hazy mist all around her so that just herself and Raul were real, and everything else had ceased to exist.

Those beautiful eyes seemed to have lost all their burning ferocity and instead were deep pools of misty gold. And when he lifted his hand and put it over hers, pressing it down onto his arm, it seemed to happen in slow motion. So did the movement of his head as he lowered it, angling it so that his mouth was aimed for hers.

And Alannah responded without thought, lifting her own face towards his, her lips parting slightly, waiting for his kiss.

'Alannah,' he said again, the warmth of his breath kissing her mouth before he did.

CHAPTER SEVEN

WHEN their lips met it was the gentleness that was totally unexpected. After the blazing passion of the night in her flat, this tenderness caught her up in a warm, swirling sea of sensation, almost seeming to draw out her soul with her breath.

Her head was swimming and her hands went up to clutch at his arms for support, and that was her first mistake. The feel of his strength underneath her seeking fingers was both a delight and a danger. A delight because she wanted to touch further, hold tighter, and a danger for exactly the same reasons. She should break away, should move fast, but her thoughts seemed to have slowed down along with her breathing, and she couldn't get her brain to send the right instructions to her body. Instead it seemed to want to cling, to cuddle, to press closer to the hard, vital heat of the man...

And that was her second mistake.

Because as soon as she pressed closer it was as if the warmth from his body had spread along her own skin. It seeped into her blood, seeming to melt down her muscles, her bones. And when she swayed on her feet his arms came round her, enfolding her, holding her tight. She was as close as she had wanted to be, clinging as she wanted to be, but in the space of a shaken heartbeat even this close was not enough.

His kiss was not enough.

Her arms slipped up around his neck, holding him, fingers caressing the softness of his hair, brushing along the exposed skin at the nape of his neck, kneading the taut muscles she found there. And all the time she was drawing his head down closer, needing the pressure of his mouth to be harder, stronger—*more*.

He took her parted lips with a skill that had her sighing, the sigh opening her mouth even more to him, letting the slide of his tongue move along the sensitive inner tissues, tasting her, enticing her, seducing her.

If she stood on tiptoe then she could increase the pressure of his mouth on hers in response to the rising heat in her blood, the singing in her nerves. Still holding his proud dark head where she wanted it with one hand, she let the fingers of the other trail down the side of his face, feeling the faint rasp of black stubble under her fingertips as she followed the line of his forceful jaw. She caught Raul's indrawn hiss of breath and smiled against his mouth as she kissed him again, this time taking her caressing fingers down his throat to slide in at the open neck of his shirt, stroking the smooth, warm flesh she found there, tracing tiny circles in the crisp body hair.

'Alannah…' Raul said again but this time her name was a growl of response against her lips.

'Mmm?' Alannah sighed, wriggling even closer,

pressing herself against him and hearing the beat of his heart kick up a notch under the powerful ribcage.

'*Dios!* You devil woman!' he muttered against her mouth and the hands that had held her held no more. Instead they roved hungrily over her body, powerful fingers curving over and cupping the soft curves of her buttocks, pulling her in even closer to the heated force of his erection.

'I only ever needed to take one look to want you more than any woman in the world. I still do.'

'Me too...I want you too.'

Alannah felt the words slip past her guard with a tiny sense of shock. Even when they'd been together, she had never been brave enough or bold enough to admit to her sexual need of this man. Oh, she'd felt it often enough. And she'd shown him in wordless, physical ways, by her responses to his kisses and his caresses, just how much she desired him. But she had never actually come right out and said it in so many words.

She could only imagine that two long years of loneliness, of missing him, missing his touch, his kiss, had driven her into a state of sensual starvation, one in which she no longer had the strength or control to impose any restraint on her tongue so that Raul's kisses had loosened even the weak grip she had on it.

Raul's kisses and the very basic, very simple need for human comfort after the loss and misery she had endured so recently. Life was too short, too precarious to be lived at a lukewarm temperature. She'd welcomed the heat of her response to Raul as a way to melt the ice that seemed to have formed around her heart, shutting her off from the world, from all emotion.

Here at least was proof that she was still very much alive—and feeling.

'You do?'

Her new openness had stunned Raul too. His dark head went back, deep-set eyes narrowing until all she could see was a tiny strip of burning gold gleaming between the thick black lashes that fringed them.

'Is this the truth?'

Some of her unexpected courage deserting her under the intense scrutiny of that smouldering gaze, Alannah felt hot colour flood her cheeks, her mouth drying sharply so that she could only nod in silent acquiescence. She wanted to look anywhere but into his eyes, unable to meet them and answer the question in them when they were fixed on hers, so she lowered her gaze hastily, meaning to stare at the floor.

Instead she found that her eyes were caught by the broad expanse of Raul's chest under the fine linen of his shirt. Where he had tugged his tie loose and unfastened a single button at the neck the tanned skin of his throat seemed impossibly dark—burnished almost—in contrast to the immaculate white and the shadow of the black, curling chest hair that showed faintly through it. The memory of how it had felt to smooth her fingertips over that hair, feeling it crisp and springy under her touch, made her swallow hard, fighting the urge to lift her hands to his chest, unbutton his shirt, to know the feeling all over again.

In an effort to resist the temptation, she forced her

eyes lower, only to find the colour rising higher in her face, heating her blood, as her gaze rested on the silver buckle and the polished black leather of the belt that fastened around the narrow waist. There was no possibility that she could be unaware of the way that the fine material of his trousers stretched tautly over the heated bulge of his erection, the force of his reaction proving physically the truth of his uninhibited claim to want her...

More than any other woman in the world?

Privately, Alannah doubted that. But for now she'd take this, she told herself. For now, simply knowing that this devastating man, the only man she'd ever wanted to sleep with, still desired her was balm to her wounded soul, a promise of delight in a world that until now had seemed to have turned completely black.

'Then what about him?' Raul pressed, the unexpectedness of the question slicing into her heated thoughts and jolting her so that her eyes flew back up to his face, a faint frown of confusion creasing the space between her finely arched brows.

'Him?' she echoed in bewilderment. 'Who? Who do you mean?'

'Who else but your other man, of course?'

Raul's tone was light, almost casual, but there was a new sharpness in his scrutiny, a watchfulness in the eyes that were once more fixed on her face, that told her that his words were meant far from casually. And in the same moment that the realisation of just what he meant hit home, the recognition of the fact that it truly mattered to him rocked her world with the sense of a blow to her head, making her thoughts spin dizzily.

'My other man…' was all she could croak, her voice deserting her as she struggled for control. 'Who…?'

His swift dark frown reproved her and she knew that he believed she was playing with him, not understanding simply for the hell of it, deliberately being provocative in order to rile him further.

'Let's get one thing straight, *querida*,' he muttered, low and harsh, 'I don't sleep with other men's women, no matter how strong the temptation.'

'Other men's women!' Alannah spluttered indignantly. 'Let me tell you that I'm no man's woman! I don't belong to anyone and—'

'Then the new lover is no longer in the picture?' Raul shot at her, the question getting under her guard like a sharp stiletto knife in her ribs.

'There is no new lover!' she flung at him then, her throat closing up in horror as she saw his dark head go back and realised what she had said and how much she had given away. She could almost see his mind going back over their last day together, reliving the scene, recalling everything she had said…

'So you walked out on him too, hmm? But perhaps you gave the poor fool more than the few months you gave me. And then…' pausing to stare deep into her eyes, he lifted a hand and ran it softly down the side of her face, smiling darkly as he watched her automatic reaction, the way she arched slightly into the caress, her eyes half closing sensually '…his loss is my gain…'

And, bending his head, he took her mouth again in

a kiss so deeply sensual that it made her head swim, had her clutching at his shoulders, crushing the fine material of his jacket under nerveless fingers as once more the tidal wave of sensation took her by storm. The heated caress of his hands, sweeping down her neck, over her shoulders, along her arms, made her shudder in pleasurable response and she pressed herself closer to the warm power of his body, needing more than such a gentle touch. Raul laughed softly, deep in his throat, and drew her in, holding her close as he tilted up her head so that he could plunder her mouth more effectively.

The hand that was at her back moved up to the V neckline of her dress, sliding in, finding the warm skin underneath and stroking softly. When he heard her murmur of delight and felt the way that the light touch made her squirm against him he dropped the hand that had been under her chin to the same sensitive area, tracing erotic patterns with his fingers outwards and downwards, moving towards the spot where her tight and swollen breasts pressed against the confines of her bra. In the moment that those tantalising fingertips brushed over the sensitised peaks under the pale green satin, Alannah gasped aloud in shocked delight to the fierce intensity of feeling his touch created, heat pooled low down between her legs and she pressed her mouth harder against his, mutely encouraging more of the arousing delight. With one hand he held her there while the other moved down the front of her dress, wrenching open the small pearly buttons that held it fastened with hungry impatience. When his hot fingers closed over the swell of her breast in the silk and lace of her bra, thumb and forefinger scissoring together to tweak the already straining nipple into stinging life, Alannah gasped again, her head falling back as she reacted to the electric jolt of pleasure that burned through her.

The movement gave Raul even more access to the front of her dress, ripping open buttons with such force that several flew away from her, bouncing off the table, the arm of the chair. Bent backwards on his supporting arm, she felt him ease one aching breast out of the silky cup of her bra, lifting it so that the pouting nipple was exposed, easily accessible to the hotly tormenting caress of his mouth.

'Raul…' His name was a crooning sound, a note of wonder and almost disbelief at the pleasure he was giving her.

She felt him half walk, half carry her part way across the room, knew the pressure of the seat of the settee at the backs of her knees before she tumbled down onto the black leather, crushed against the cushions by the weight of Raul's body following her.

'You are eternal temptation,' Raul muttered against her neck, where his burning mouth was now working another sort of magic, one that involved the delicately erotic patterns his tongue was tracing over her skin, making her writhe in delight. 'And I have never ever been able to resist temptation.'

Each word was punctuated with another kiss, hard, demanding, possessive. Making her his, stamping her with his brand.

'Never…'

And, now that she had come so near and yet so far so many times, the flames that were waiting to engulf Alannah's body, her mind, flared and raged out of control in the space of a frantic heartbeat. She didn't have time to think or even to breathe as Raul crushed her under his weight.

His mouth was fierce on hers, his hands urgent, burning as they explored every shivering inch of her. Those wicked fingers had now opened the front of her dress right down to her navel so that they could slide in further, pushing under the yielding elastic at the top of her knickers, reaching down to where the need pulsed hardest, making her whimper in hungry response.

'No…' he muttered when he was forced to snatch in a rough, ragged breath—it was either that or suffocate.

No? The question sounded in her head; she didn't have the strength or the ability to actually voice it, let alone understand the harsh-voiced Spanish snarled against the side of her neck. How could he mean no when she wanted this so badly and she could have sworn…?

'Not like this,' Raul responded impatiently. 'Not here—the bedroom…'

'Yes…'

Alannah managed a gasp of sound. She had no time for more because as soon as she had spoken her lips were claimed again and Raul lifted her right off her feet and bundled her out in the direction she had indicated so fast that her head spun. His mouth was still hard against hers, weaving a sensual magic with his lips and his tongue, and the hands that held her were clamped around her hips, managing to caress her in a way that stoked the fires of her need at the same time that they lifted her and carried her, in the direction of the bedroom.

'This will have to go!'

Impatience had got the better of him and he propped her up against the wall again, taking the now loosened dress by the hem and wrenching it upwards. For a moment Alannah was blinded by the green cloth over her face but then he pulled it free again and tossed it aside, careless of the way that it landed on the polished wooden floor in a crumpled heap.

'Better…'

Dark eyes dropped to the spill of her breasts from the confines of the pale green satin and he drew in a deep, uneven breath.

'Much better.'

Alannah's own breath was snatched in as he curved his big hands under each breast, cupping and lifting them to the caress of his mouth, the wicked, tormenting flicker of his hot tongue. Almost unable to bear it, Alannah writhed against the wall, colour flushing her face, heat flooding her body, the intensity of arousal so sharp it was like a stab of pain.

'Raul…'

It was a moan of protest—or encouragement, and even she couldn't have said which. With her back still against the wall, she edged her way inch by inch towards the door at the end of the corridor that led to the bedroom. The burn of his touch on her sensitised skin was wonderful, and the flare of need it woke inside seared through every nerve, every cell of her body. But if he dragged this out any longer then she was going to go up in flames like a forest fire, raging through paper-dry undergrowth.

'Raul—please…'

A laugh, low, dark, triumphant, greeted her plea and, catching hold of her again, keeping her still with the strength of one arm around her, Raul captured her mouth, subjecting it to a sensually tormenting onslaught as his free hand swiftly and efficiently dealt with the clasp of her bra, freeing it and tossing it aside, somewhere in the general direction of the already discarded dress.

The feel of his hands on the bare skin of her breasts was almost more than she could take. Her head went back against the wall, a low, wild moan escaping her, and she sagged at the knees, coming close to collapse in delight.

'Raul—*please*…!'

Another laugh, even rougher this time, sounded low in his throat as he pressed a line of hot kisses along her shoulder and into the small hollow at the base of her neck. And all the time those wicked, knowing, tantalising hands played havoc with her senses as they touched and stroked and teased and tormented the stinging tips of her breasts, one moment gentle, then tugging on the swollen nipples until she felt she might actually pass out with the force of the sensations she was feeling.

But then suddenly it seemed that Raul lost all patience. No longer prepared to anticipate, to delay, to drag out the pleasure for a moment longer, he gave a low growl and snatched her up into his arms, swinging her high as he strode the few metres down the corridor to the bedroom, kicking open the door and carrying her in.

Marching over to the bed, he dropped her onto it with little ceremony, obviously impatient now, nearing the end of his control just as she had almost lost hers. Eyes that were black with passion locked with Alannah's as he stripped off his clothes, letting the elegantly tailored suit, the crisp white shirt fall where they would as he tossed them aside without any concern.

And Alannah couldn't look anywhere else. She didn't want to look anywhere else. She was transfixed by the sight of the fabulous body that he was revealing, each discarded item exposing another part of the male beauty that was Raul Marcín. He was broad and strong, with straight, powerful shoulders and torso, his chest hazed with the black body hair she had glimpsed so faintly before. Exposed like this, it was darker than ever, curling and crisp, then arrowing down past his narrow waist to disappear into the waistband of his trousers.

She might have thought that as she lay there, with no touch, no kiss to stoke the fires of need he had awoken, those fires might ebb, but the truth was that the opposite was happening. Every inch of tanned olive skin that was revealed made her pulse beat stronger, harder; her blood burn hotter. Now she felt she understood just why she had never been able to replace this man in her mind and in her heart. The truth was simply that there was no one else for her; no one who could match him against her personal blueprint for the perfect man. In the few short months that they had been together he had stamped his brand on her as surely as if she had been some long-ago slave, marked as her owner's possession; his to do with as he would. And nothing had changed.

When black boxer shorts were his only clothing he came back to her, bending over the bed to take her lips in a long, lingering kiss that sparked off once again all the sensations that had driven her to distraction before. Hungrily she reached up, fastening her hands around his broad shoulders, wanting to draw him down to her, but Raul stilled her with a touch, pressing her back against the pillows while he eased the small green slip of her underwear from her body. The next moment he had pressed his mouth to the smooth flesh his hands had exposed, kissing a trail of fire the length of her body.

'*Dios*, but I need this.'

Raul's voice was raw, thickened by the hunger that she could feel tensing his body; the same hunger that was burning between her legs, making her shift restlessly on the bed.

'Me too…'

Perhaps if she soothed him, stroked him in the same way that he was touching her then he would relent and give her the satisfaction she craved. But when she smoothed her hands over his hot, bronzed skin it seemed to have the opposite effect of soothing. Instead she saw the feverish glitter of hunger in his eyes, the red slash of colour on those high carved cheekbones and heard his breathing coming rough and ragged as he fought for control.

A control she didn't want.

And when his kisses caressed her breasts, moving over the soft curves until they found the pouting pink nipple, then she could hardly find the strength to bear it.

'Raul—please—come to me…'

Her fingers fumbling in their haste, she tugged at the black boxer shorts, hearing his harsh intake of breath as he helped her with them, shrugging himself out of his last item of clothing. And then at last he was right with her, his hot body heavy on top of her, his hair-roughened legs pushing hers apart, opening her to him.

'Oh, yes… Yes…' Alannah sighed her delight, holding him tight against her, parting her legs even more so that they were either side of his narrow hips, giving him access to the innermost core of her body.

Knowing fingers stroked the exposed flesh, brushed the small, swollen centre of her desire, making her moan aloud and shiver in a response that almost took her over the edge. Almost, but not far enough. Once more her hands clutched at his wide shoulders, urging him closer, closer. And now at least she heard the breath hiss through his teeth as he abandoned all attempt at restraint and buried himself in her yearning body in one long, powerful thrust.

'Alannah…'

'Raul—yes…'

Their voices clashed on the night air, echoing wildly in the silent, shadowed room.

But even as the sound of her name died away she knew that something had changed. Something in her reaction, some tiny quiver in her voice at the sting of pain, some momentary tension that she couldn't restrain, had given her away. Raul's long body stilled, tautening sharply as he fought for control, and the dark head that had been thrown back in uncontrolled response now came forward again, golden eyes searching her face, looking for the answer to the question that clearly burned in his mind.

'*Still?*' he said and the single word encompassed a world of meaning, of disbelief, of shock. 'Still so innocent? But how…?'

She knew his eyes were on her, knew that that intently burning gaze was searching her face, looking for the answer he wanted, the answer she didn't know how to give him—didn't dare to give him. And so she kept her own eyes tight shut and used her hands to distract him, wanting to divert him from the realisation that she had still kept the virginity he had once prized so highly, stroking softly so that he writhed under her touch.

'How doesn't matter. It doesn't matter,' she assured him, low-voiced and urgent.

She didn't want him to think of it, didn't want it to make him hesitate, perhaps even—oh, dear heaven, no—perhaps even make him stop. He couldn't stop now or she felt that her heart would burst with the need that was pounding through her untried body. She didn't need experience, or knowledge, to sense that something very special, something spectacular was so very close, almost within reach.

'Alannah…' Raul muttered, thick and rough, but she shook her head in denial of his concern, her body moving restlessly under his, opening even further.

'Nothing matters—but this—but now—but us…'

And with a gentle touch, the deliberately provocative movements of her body that every feminine instinct taught her how to use, she fought to divert his thoughts on to other, more pleasurable paths. She knew she had succeeded when she heard his groan of surrender, felt the long body that covered her tense in a new and different way.

'Yes,' she whispered close against his ear. 'Yes—please, Raul—please make me yours…'

Beyond the windows, the day was cold and grey, the dark clouds threatening rain once again. But here, in their own confined and private little world, there was nothing but heat and hunger, the burn of desire and the delight of touch, of deep, sensual, wonderful movement. A heat that grew and grew, building higher and higher with each glorious movement, each kiss, each caress that took her further and further from reality and into the throes of sensation that closed over her like a tidal wave, swamping her. Abandoning herself completely, she surrendered to it, gave herself up to the wonder of it until she lost all sense of anything but the soaring, blinding, blazing yearning for completion.

And suddenly she was no longer yearning but exploding, whirling and soaring high out of the world and into a delirium of pleasure that exploded in her mind, devastating it totally. Somewhere, a long, long way away, she heard Raul's wild cry of delight as he followed her over the edge and their bodies clenched tightly together, frozen, suspended, clinging on to the last shuddering aftershocks of delight.

Only when they had ebbed away did she sigh and let herself collapse back on the bed, her breathing raw and ragged, her chest heaving, her body replete, her mind numb. And Raul came with her, his long body sprawled over hers in total abandonment as he dragged in heavy, almost painful breaths in the struggle to regain some sort of control. His powerful frame was slicked with sweat, his head limp and heavy against her breast. She could feel his heartbeat still racing hard against his ribcage, in matching time to her own.

It took a long time before his breathing finally slowed and with a long, contented sigh he rolled off her to lie on his back with one arm flung up across his eyes.

'*Dios*,' he muttered hoarsely. 'If I had known it would be like this I would never have let you go…'

She'd always known, Alannah acknowledged in the privacy of her thoughts. She had thought that she'd forgotten—or tried to forget—just what an effect Raul had always had on her, the aching yearning, the blazing need that he could awaken simply by existing, it seemed. But the truth was that it was all just there, right below the surface, needing only a touch, a kiss, to set light to the still smouldering embers of her need for him and she had gone up in flames. Totally at his command.

And she had to face it now that it would always be that way. That she would never be free of Raul, but always tied to him, always in thrall to him and to her own need of him. It was a need that no one night, no thousands of nights could ever hope to appease. Instead it would take the rest of her life and she still wouldn't be free of her hunger for him.

But for now at least that hunger was appeased, her body satiated. For now she felt settled, at ease, and as Raul turned on his side his strong arms came round her, safe and secure. Her body ached in so many places, but it was a wonderful, satisfied ache, one that matched the delight that still made her glow in every nerve, every inch of her skin. What had happened between them this evening had reminded both of them of what they had once shared. Even if this was all that she meant to Raul then surely from now on things had to be better.

At her side Raul stirred and, reaching out a hand, pulled up the duvet and flung it over her, enclosing them both in a soft, warm cave of down, cosy and snug. He was lying behind her now, with the length of his body pressed against hers, legs tangled together.

She cuddled closer, feeling his arms holding her tight. In the warmth and security of his embrace, she felt her eyes grow heavy, droop closed, warm waves of tiredness washing over her. For the first time in five days she felt the tension that had been with her every second slowly ease from her.

She was drifting away, almost going under, when Raul's mood suddenly changed. He sighed, flung himself on his back, folding one arm behind his head as he stared up at the ceiling.

'Alannah…'

Whatever else he was about to say was drowned out by the sound of a loud, intrusive rap at the door.

CHAPTER EIGHT

'WHAT?'

Alannah started sharply, turning in the bed towards Raul as he froze, looking down into her upturned face, seeing the way her deep green eyes widened in shock, her face losing colour.

'Who…?' Her lips formed the word silently in the same moment that they heard a voice on the other side of the door.

'Porter, sir. Come to collect your bag.'

'Infierno!'

Raul's gaze, still unfocused from the storm of passion that had assailed him, went to where the case he had packed such a short time earlier still stood by the door in the sitting room.

With another muttered curse in his native language he flung back the covers, jacknifed up and out of the bed, snatching up the shirt and trousers he had tossed aside so recently. It was the work of seconds to pull them on. A quick glance back down at her face saw the shock and consternation that was written there as

Alannah frantically pulled the covers up high over her exposed breasts.

'Wait here. I'll deal with this.'

Raking his hands though his ruffled hair in a hasty attempt to smooth away the evidence of her clutching fingers, he hurried from the room, shutting the door carefully behind him.

It was as he crossed the sitting room that he noticed how Alannah's shoes had fallen onto the floor in the heat of their passion earlier and now lay tumbled on the carpet. Recalling the look of panic on her face and knowing that she would hate it if anyone realised what had happened, he kicked them out of sight under the settee as he headed for the door.

After handing over the case and a tip, the generosity of which made the man blink in stunned delight, he dismissed the porter thankfully, leaning back against the door and closing his eyes momentarily with a deep sigh. But even as relief at having dealt with one situation relaxed his shoulders for a moment, the thought of another yet to be sorted out had him tensing up again.

What the devil had just happened?

He had vowed never to see Alannah Redfern again; never to let her back into his life. And yet as soon as fate had forced them together he had acted as blindly, as stupidly, as crazily as some horny adolescent at the mercy of his hormones.

He had been off balance, true. This week had left his brain clouded, his emotions raw, but that was no excuse. One kiss, one touch and he had been in the power of his libido and it was as if all the time he had spent maturing, learning control, becoming a man and not a wayward boy, had been stripped away, leaving him a prey to his most basic, most primitive desires in a second.

But then Alannah had always been able to do that to him. From the moment they had first met, less than three years before, he hadn't been able to keep his hands off her. Her body called to his in the way that no other woman had ever done, before or since, and he had never felt so out of control, so much as if his life wasn't his own. He hadn't liked it then—and he liked it one hell of a lot less now.

Because nothing was as he had believed it to be.

Last time he had proposed marriage to her. And she had laughed in his face and walked away to be with another man—or so she had claimed. But the woman he had taken to bed just now had been a virgin, as innocent as she had been two years ago.

Which meant that two days ago, when he had believed that she was coming on to him in order to get what she wanted from him, in fact...

In fact, what?

Pushing both hands through his hair again, he turned back into the room, and, seeing the mobile phone still lying on the table where he had slammed it, picked it up and pressed the speed-dial button for Carlos. When the chauffeur answered he spoke quickly to his driver, keeping it as brief as possible. Alannah would be waiting and he was impatient to get back to her.

He didn't think he had been very long, but by the time he opened the door into the bedroom it was obvious that he had taken too much time. And Alannah's mood had changed as a result.

She was no longer in the bed where he'd left her. Instead, she was up and had dressed again…at least, as well as she could, with the buttons—as many of them as were left intact—fastened up and her dress pulled together where she could close the gaps that revealed the pale green silk and lace of her bra, the peachy tones of her flesh.

But it was her expression that concerned him most. She was sitting on the edge of the bed, the stiffness of her body, spine straight, head held high, and the frozen, stiff-mouthed, distant-eyed look that told of a very different frame of mind from that of the ardent, sensual woman he had had in his arms no more than a few minutes before.

Silently and savagely cursing the ill-timed appearance of the porter, Raul hid his frustration behind a smile.

'He's gone now. You can relax.'

Relaxing looked like the last thing on her mind as she got up from the bed, fingers clutching tightly at the front of her dress, dragging it closed where it gaped worst.

'If you'd arrange for that car to take me home now,' she said in a small, stiff, oh-so-typically-English voice, 'I'd be very much obliged.'

Raul's breath hissed in through his teeth in a sound of fierce exasperation.

'And I'd be obliged if you'd stop freezing up and come back here so that I can kiss you again—'

Green eyes clashed with gold, hers so defiant that he felt he could almost see the sparks flashing from them and snapping in the air. Oh, damn that porter to hell! His timing just couldn't have been worse.

'I don't think so—I don't think that this is a good idea.'

'You don't think!' Raul exploded. 'You don't… No, look…' he amended hastily, seeing the way she stepped back at his outburst, the clouded look that had come into her eyes. 'Alannah, *querida*—just stop this nonsense. Just don't think. It doesn't help matters.'

'Help what?'

'Thinking just gets in the way—what we have doesn't need thought, or sense, it just needs this…'

He reached for her, wanting to kiss her back into the hot, hungry state she had been in just moments before, The hot, hungry, *demanding* state where she had been clutching at his arms, his back, his hair, anything she could get her hands on to hold him closer, bringing him as tight against her body as he could be. But she dodged away from his hand, moving to the far side of the room, where she faced him, stubborn defiance stamped into every line of her face.

'This isn't going to happen again,' she flung at him, stamping her foot in emphasis, though because she was barefooted and the carpet was soft and thick the result was obviously not what she had hoped for. The glare she turned on him warned him not to laugh, so he swallowed down his amusement though some of it still lingered in his voice.

'Of course it's going to happen again. We can't stop it—we don't have any say in the matter.'

'On the contrary—I have plenty of say in the matter and what I'm saying is no.'

'That's not what you were saying just now—in there.'

A tilt of his dark head indicated the abandoned bed, where the covers and pillows were still crumpled and in disarray.

'Are you going to claim that—?'

'I'm not claiming anything,' Alannah cut in on him sharply. 'Only that I want to go home. And you have a plane to catch. And I have no intention of being slotted in for a quick tumble to while away the time between now and the point where you have to leave. So if you will please call your driver…'

'I've called him already,' Raul pointed out.

If her problem was that she thought he was going to spare her only a minimum of time then she couldn't be more wrong. He had no intention of rushing this. There was no way in hell that she was going to be just a 'quick tumble'.

'And told him not to come at the time we originally arranged but to leave it until I called him. But if you're worried about the plane then—'

'I don't give a damn about the plane! I'm well aware of the fact that Don High and Mighty Il Duque Raul Marcín has the power and the money to have a private plane at his beck and call so that all you have to do is snap your fingers and the pilot is ready to fly as and when you command. But you needn't think that you can do the same with me.'

Now he couldn't hold back the laughter. This was just too ridiculous.

'I don't have to snap my fingers—just use them to touch you, and you'll be mine to do exactly as I command.'

He moved forward, hand raised, fingers spread, to show her just how stupid this all was. But she started like a nervous horse, edging backwards again, and this time her hand actually came up and dashed his aside with a sharp slap before she whirled away from him, moving swiftly to the other side of the room.

'Don't you dare! I don't want this!'

'You don't want…'

This time his laughter was cold, hard, no trace of humour in it anywhere.

'You little liar,' he said in a low, deadly tone. 'You wanted it only too much just now—so what the hell has changed your mind?'

'I'll tell you what's changed my mind.'

Her chin came up, her eyes flashing even more, and Raul couldn't help but be distracted by the way that the unevenness of her breathing made the precariously fastened dress gape even more, exposing the smooth swell of her breasts, rising and falling in the most provocative way.

'Please do.'

'*You* changed it!'

'I did? And how?'

'Isn't it obvious? You come sauntering back in here, clearly expecting that I'll be waiting for you—just dying to finish what we started! I wouldn't be at all surprised if you didn't think that I might have stayed naked and ready in this bed—' a wild gesture with one hand indicated the bed that now stood between them '—to save time!'

'I told you—'

'Yes, I know what you told me. You told me that you had already phoned your driver—that you were so sure of your conquest that you didn't bother to check whether I was still—still up for it—before you postponed your travel plans so that you could have a quick—'

'Don't you dare!' Raul broke in on a roar of fury. 'You know it wasn't like that.'

'Do I? Do I really? So tell me, Raul, just what was it like?'

'You wanted it as much as I did.'

'*Wanted.* You're right there, Raul. The word is *wanted.* Past. I might have wanted—wanted you—but you made one big mistake. You gave me time to think…time to have second—and third, and, believe me, fourth—thoughts about this. And I came to the conclusion—the only wise, the only sensible conclusion—that I do *not* want anything more to do with you. I should never have come here—I would never have come here if it hadn't been for your damn phone and I've given you that back—so now it's goodbye, and this time it's for ever!'

Hell and damnation, no! Rejection of everything she said was like a red haze in Raul's mind. It couldn't stop now. Not like this. This wasn't going to happen again. She wasn't going to walk out on him all over again, not when he had just rediscovered that sensual satisfaction—the deepest, most perfect satisfaction—that he only ever found with her.

He'd tried to find it elsewhere—tried for two long, frustrating years. And no woman had ever even come close. He would do anything, pay any price, resort to any blackmail, just to have this woman where she belonged—in his bed.

'You're not leaving.'

'No? Just watch me.'

She flounced past him, tossing that glorious red hair as she did so. He knew from the flashing, sideways, wary look she gave him that she expected him to try and grab at her, hold her back, so he derived a dark satisfaction from wrong-footing her, instead leaning back against the wall, folding his arms across his chest and watching her, waiting a nicely calculated moment.

'Don't you think that you'd be better off with something on your feet?' he drawled at last, just in time to stop her halfway across the room.

'What?'

Alannah stopped dead, half turned back, then looked down at her bare feet, pale against the deep burgundy colour of the carpet.

'Where—?' she began, but Raul ignored her and cut across her indignant question.

'And were you really planning to walk through the hotel—and all the way back to your flat—dressed, or perhaps I should say undressed, like that?'

As he spoke he let his cool gaze slide from her angry face and down over her body, lingering deliberately at the spot where three buttons were missing and the front of her dress gaped wide over the lace of her bra.

She looked a total mess, Alannah admitted, while he…well, his clothes were faintly crumpled from their time on the floor and on anyone else that should have looked untidy, even messy, but somehow on Raul they had a very different effect. He looked ruffled, relaxed— and real. Light-years away from his normal smooth, sleek, business-suited self—and very, very sexy. It was impossible to look at him, at the expanse of broad chest exposed by the still unbuttoned shirt, and not think of how just a short time before she had lain with her head pillowed on that chest, the crisp dark hairs tickling her cheek as she heard his breathing slow, the thundering of his heart gradually ease as he too recovered from the wild ferocity of their lovemaking.

Gasping in shock, she felt the hot colour flood her cheeks as she grabbed at her dress again, pulling the pieces back together as closely as she could. But holding it there meant that she had no way of opening the door. And she still had to find…

'*Where* are my shoes?'

Close to something like panic, she scanned the room, searching for any sign of the pale leather pumps she had worn on her way here. She couldn't see them anywhere.

'Raul…'

'Alannah…'

He levered himself up from his position against the wall, and she watched warily as he came towards her slowly.

'Why don't you sit down for a moment and let's talk about this?'

He sounded so calm, so reasonable that her mouth

actually fell open and she gaped at him in blank bewilderment. Whatever had happened to Mr 'Of course this is going to happen again'? Was he actually prepared to be *reasonable*? Or was he just hiding his darker side behind this suddenly civilised veneer?

She had no way of knowing and the truth was that her own thought processes were far from trustworthy. She felt as if she had been at the eye of a tropical storm ever since she had come to Raul's hotel room, picked up and whirled around, battered by a fury of conflicting feelings. Even now, her body still ached with the hungry passion that had raged through her in the moment when Raul had taken her in his arms and kissed her. The honest truth was that even as she'd collapsed into sated exhaustion from his lovemaking a weak, greedy part of her had already been anticipating something more.

If the knock at the door had never happened, or if it had come a minute or two later, then there would have been no going back. She would have turned to Raul once more and if he had taken her into his arms and kissed her again then she would have gone to him, opened herself to him willingly and eagerly. All it would have taken was another kiss, another caress from Raul to stoke the fires that she knew had only died down, not died away. She knew she would have been incapable of saying no—that she wouldn't have *wanted* to say no—and once more Raul would have made her his, stamped his possession on her without a thought.

But the knock at the door had come. It had broken through the burning haze that had filled her mind, snatching her out of the delirium of need and right back into harsh reality in the space of a couple of seconds.

She had waited, shivering in heated reaction, in the bedroom, listening to him dealing with the porter, handing over the case, heard the door shut. Every nerve in her body had still been so alive, so awake that if he had come to her then she still wouldn't have been able to think. If he had walked through that door right then she knew with a sense of despair that she would have gone straight into his arms, drawn to him like a fragile needle was brought close by the fierce pull of the strongest magnet. She would not have been able to stay away. All he would have had to do was to say 'Come', and she would have obeyed. So great was the spell he had cast over her.

But he hadn't come to her. He hadn't opened his arms. He hadn't said 'Come'. Instead he had paused, picked up the phone and called Carlos.

And suddenly it was as if the bottom had dropped out of her world. Her heart had plummeted, twisting as it went and every last trace of heat had ebbed from her body, leaving her shivering in a very different way.

'I've called him already,' Raul had said. 'And told him not to come at the time we originally arranged but to leave it until I called him.'

But she didn't need him to tell her that. She didn't care what he had said, or, rather, exactly how he had phrased it. She had heard him through the door. Heard how, once he had got rid of the porter, his first instinct had been to pick up the phone, call his driver. She'd heard the name Carlos, and even if she hadn't understood the rest of the fast, autocratic Spanish, she had known only too well what was going on.

Because by then realisation had already hit home. And realisation had brought with it a heavy dose of cold reality—the sort of reality that she couldn't dodge away from, couldn't avoid, no matter how much she might want to.

While she was still dealing with the aftershocks of the hurricane of feeling that had swept her up, while her body still trembled in stunned delight at the sensations she had experienced and her mind whirled and spun from the force of feeling she had been subjected to, Raul had been calmly and coolly getting on with his life, dealing with the practicalities.

The practicalities of packing and checking out of his hotel room—leaving England, going back to Spain.

And leaving her behind.

Well, what had she expected, poor stupid fool that she was? Had she really thought that there might be more for her than this? That he might actually want more than he had just had—her willing body under his in the bed? Could she really think that once he had made love to her…had sex with her—she forced herself to look at what had just happened as it truly was—even the hotly passionate, wildly fulfilling sex that they had both enjoyed, he would put all his plans on hold, wanting to stay with her, wanting to have her in his future?

If she'd even allowed herself to dream of that then she would have been desperately disappointed. No sooner had he had his way than Raul had called his chauffeur, sorting out the arrangements for his journey back to Spain as if nothing had happened.

Because to him, nothing had happened. Lying alone in that bed, with her passionate responses cooling as rapidly as the sheets that Raul had just left, Alannah had had to force herself to face the real truth. Two years before, when he had believed her worth marrying, even if her value to him had been only that she would be his virgin bride and bear him the children he so desperately longed for, Raul had always held back; always restrained his hungry passion for her.

He would not make love to her until they were married, he'd said, and he'd held to that no matter how hard it had obviously been for him. Until tonight.

If she had needed any proof of how little she meant to him then it had been there in the way he had taken her here, in this bed that she now could no longer bear to stay in but had flung herself out of, grabbing at her clothes and rushing into them in miserable desperation.

She had handed herself to Raul on a plate and he had taken everything she had offered. He didn't want to want her but he couldn't stop himself. And as soon as he had had what he wanted he had been making plans to leave. Assuming that what had happened had meant as little to her as it had to him.

And then he had strolled back into the room, large as life and twice as arrogant, assuming something else. Assuming that she would be sitting there—preferably *lying* there—waiting for him to take up where he had left off. So that he could deal with the problem as quickly as possible and be on his way.

And, fool that she was, she *had* been waiting. She had stayed in that room, silent and—damn it— obedient to his wishes! No wonder he had thought that he could take what he wanted from her, that she would pander to his every desire. If she had had any sense she would have snatched the opportunity while the porter was at the door to come out of the bedroom, sweep past him and out of the door before he had a chance to protest or complain. And the thought of him trying to explain why a half-dressed woman with no shoes might need to get out of the hotel suite as swiftly as possible brought a certain grim satisfaction to her mind.

'Why should I want to sit down? And what could we possibly have to *talk* about?'

'I have a proposition I want to put to you.'

'A proposition?'

Alannah eyed him warily. He still looked calm— worryingly so. What had happened to the hotly passionate lover of just a few short minutes before—and the arrogant swine who had declared 'I don't have to snap my fingers—just use them to touch you, and you'll be mine to do exactly as I command'? It seemed that in the space of just a few brief moments Raul Marcín had been at least three different men, if not more. There was the hotly passionate lover, the man who with calm good humour and spectacular arrogance had dismissed her protests as unnecessary and now here, it seemed, was the businessman who had a *proposition* to put to her. And she had no way of beginning to guess just which of them was the real person.

'What sort of a proposition?'

Why was she even asking? She didn't want to spend any more time in his company. It was too upsetting, too disquieting, too dangerous to her peace of mind and her sense of self-preservation. She wanted to get out of here.

Didn't she?

But just as her mind threw the question at her she knew that she had already hesitated for too long even to convince herself. The angry impetus that had fired her, driving her feet towards the door, refusing to let her look back or even consider any other possible alternative, had seeped away from her, her yearning senses were already reminding her of what they were missing and the nagging ache of frustration low down in her body was almost too much to bear.

'Sit down and I'll tell you.'

Raul gestured towards the settee but the memories the big leather sofa held were too strong, too devastating for her to be comfortable. So she deliberately chose another seat, one of the big armchairs that matched the settee, and sat there stiffly, legs primly together, her hands clasped on her knees. She was painfully aware of the way that there must be a huge contrast between her position and the state of her tumbled hair, the still gaping dress.

'So I'm sitting—tell me what you want to talk about. About this—prop…'

To her consternation and horror she couldn't actually find the right word in her thoughts. The one her bruised mind kept throwing at her was 'proposal'—*this proposal*. And she knew that proposing was the furthest thing from Raul's thoughts.

But what truly scared her was the fact that she had actually thought of anything to do with proposals and marriage in connection with Raul at all. That was the last thing she wanted. The last thing she…

Rational thoughts evaporated, driven away by an explosion of disbelief inside her head as Raul came close—and went down on one knee just before her.

'R-Raul…' she began but the heat of panic inside her head dried her mouth and she had to slick her tongue desperately across her lips in an attempt to get any control over her voice again.

Panic? Or did she mean anticipation? Either way she could only be grateful that she hadn't actually been able to say anything when he turned slightly and fished under the base of the settee, pulling out first one and then the other of her flat cream ballerina pumps.

'Your shoes, *querida*,' he said on a note of irony. 'Here, let me help you…'

When his hand fastened around her ankle to lift her foot, his touch was warm and gentle and she shivered in a contradictory response to the heat that radiated out from where he held her. With care and skill he slipped her foot into the shoe and then reached for the other one, helped her into that one too.

'There you are, Cenicienta.'

Cenicienta—Cinderella. From somewhere came the memory of Raul telling her of a children's opera with that name. But when her mind made the dangerous connection between Raul and Cinderella's hero in the fairy story, she forced it away from the foolish path down which it wanted to go.

The pad of his thumb smoothed along the top of her foot, leaving a trail of fire in its wake as he smiled up into her uncertain eyes.

'Now you can run away as soon as you like.'

If anything was going to bring her back down to reality with a bang then it was that snide comment, and every last temptation to imagine Raul as Prince Charming evaporated in a flash.

'I was not running away! So if you have any stupid ideas of coming after me with one shoe, to see if it fits, then you can forget them.'

Why wouldn't her voice work in the way she wanted it to? Why did it come and go in the most peculiar way? And there was the strangest thickness in the back of her throat that was forcing her to swallow uncomfortably. It couldn't have anything to do with tears, could it?

But the pricking at the backs of her eyes told its own story. As did the blurring of Raul's face. She wasn't going to give in to them, though. Swallowing hard, she forced her chin up, her mouth firming. So what if it was just a little too tight to be called *firm* and might actually merit the description *clamped shut* instead? No tear had fallen and now her eyes felt burning dry and gritty. Not in the least bit comfortable but at least she was safe from giving away her foolish, naïve dreams.

'And you're definitely no Prince Charming. So what exactly do you want? And please get up from your knees. You look ridiculous—and it's not as if you're about to ask me to marry you or anything like that.'

'Why not?' Raul astounded her by saying and he sat back to stare her straight in the face. 'Marriage might not be a bad idea, after all.'

CHAPTER NINE

'WHAT?'

Strangely, in spite of the fact that she was now looking slightly down at him, his position in no way diminished him, and the expression—or, rather, the total lack of expression—on his features made her shiver faintly inside. But in a very different way from the sensual reaction that had run through her body before. Now she felt both hot and cold as if in the grip of some nasty fever.

And what she had heard—thought she'd heard—had to be part of the delirium.

'What—what did you say?'

'That marriage might not be a bad idea. In fact…'

To Alannah's shock and horror he moved again, coming back onto one knee. He reached for her hand and, nerveless with disbelief, she didn't even have the brain power to snatch it back in time.

'Alannah, would you consider marrying me?'

If what she had heard before had been ridiculous—then this was totally impossible. It couldn't be happening. Not only did Raul seem to be proposing, but he was also actually doing so in a far more traditional and, some would say, romantic way than the first time. Then he had been supremely casual, almost flippant— 'I think we should get married; how about it?' Now he was actually down on one knee.

Except that this time he wasn't serious—he couldn't possibly be serious. The cruel irony of that stabbed at her as she struggled to stammer out some sort of a response.

'Mar— I— Why would I want to marry you? *Why* would you even ask?'

'I would have thought that was obvious.'

'Not to me it isn't!'

Nothing about this was obvious. Nothing at all. She could see no reason why Raul should suddenly start offering marriage proposals—proposals that made no sort of sense that she could find.

Except…

Oh, dear God, no…

It wasn't possible, was it? The fear that had just slid into her mind, cold and sneaking and chilling her soul with a terrible sense of creeping desolation.

Of course. Raul had never expected to find that she was still a virgin; never thought that he would be the first, and outside of the marriage he had once offered her. And Raul was a true Spanish aristocrat, proud to the bone and imbued with the high standards, the fierce sense of honour that came down through his ancestry.

She couldn't bear to think that he was only proposing out of that sense of honour. That once again the idea of marriage came with no sense of love, only the most pragmatic reasons for even thinking of it. How could she ever even consider accepting it when she knew that one day, inevitably, he would come to feel trapped in such an arrangement, maybe even fall in love and want someone else? And then he would resent her, grow to hate her for coming between him and his true desires.

She wanted desperately to pull her hand away. In spite of the warmth of his clasp around it, her fingers felt like ice. But when she tried to withdraw his grip around her tightened, holding her captive.

'But I don't want to marry you,' she managed in a strange little croaky voice, needing to hide the pain of her real thoughts from him. 'Marriage is for people who love each other.'

'But love doesn't have to come into it. What about wanting—passion? You can't deny the passion be-tween us.'

'I'm not denying it…'

She felt as if she was fighting for her life. As if cold dark waters were threatening to close over her head and she was going down, down, down under them.

'But it isn't enough to make me want to tie myself to you…'

'How about as a way of healing?'

'Healing?'

In spite of a struggle to impose restraint on it Alannah found that her foolish heart had lifted on a breathless little dance. Could he possibly mean…?

'Both our families have suffered terrible losses. Not just in the present but they've lost part of the future as well. You've lost a brother. I've lost a sister. And my father and your mother have both lost a longed-for grandchild.'

And then she knew exactly where he was going. She should have known it, of course, but just for a moment she had allowed herself to let the hope—the dream—of something else slip into her mind. And because of that the disappointment was so much harder to bear.

'And your point is?'

Raul's sigh was one of pure exasperation. How could she possibly be so stupid? the look in his eyes said. Surely it was obvious…?

It was obvious but she was still going to make him spell it out. If he was actually proposing marriage with the cold-blooded purpose she thought was in his mind then he was going to have to say it.

'We can heal our families, Alannah. We can't replace what they've lost but we can offer them a future. A future with a grandchild to look forward to. There's one way we can give them that.'

This time Alannah did find the strength to snatch her hand away from his grasp. She couldn't bear to have him touching her any longer.

'We?' she croaked.

'Of course.'

Raul got up from his place on the carpet and came to sit on the arm of her chair. Now he was looking down at her, and the change in his position made an amazing difference to the way she was feeling. Now he seemed to tower over her, his big body imposing and somehow intimidating, for all that he showed no anger or any intention of using his powerful strength against her. Right now it was the force of his mind that she feared most. The ruthless determination to do what he believed was right—to follow the path he wanted, and to take others along that path with him whether they wanted to go or not.

Of course. She had forgotten—how could she have forgotten?—the dynastic pride and the emphasis on tradition, the line of inheritance that drove this family. Hadn't it been the only reason that Raul had wanted to marry her in the first place—to provide his family with an heir, a new Marquez Marcín to inherit the estate, to carry on the line?

'Who else is there?'

'You could find someone else. There must be lots of women who would want to be Dona Marquez Marcín. You've never had any trouble attracting women before—there were dozens before you met me and, if the reports in the papers are anything to go by, there have been dozens of dozens since.'

'Don't believe everything you read in the papers,' Raul snarled, a dark frown drawing his black brows together. 'And if I'd wanted them, don't you think I'd have chosen one of them by now? There's only one woman I want—and don't you dare say "who?"'

'Oh, come on!'

The nerves in her stomach twisting into tight, painful knots, Alannah got to her feet in a rush and almost danced away from the chair, she was so much on edge. This couldn't be happening. It really couldn't.

How could Raul believe that she could accept such

a cold-blooded, cold-hearted proposal? At least the first time he had asked her he had covered up his true intentions by pretending he wanted to marry her for herself. She had even told herself that it didn't matter that he had never said he loved her—obviously he must do if he wanted to marry her.

It was only later when she had overheard him talking to his father—telling the old man that he had done his duty and found a suitable bride; that he would now be able to provide the grandchild and the heir that Matias so longed for—that she had begun to realise that there was more to it than she had believed. And when she had challenged him, he hadn't troubled to hide the truth.

'Of course I want a child!' he'd declared. 'Why else would I want to marry you?'

'You can't possibly really want to marry me!' she protested now. 'You said you hated me.'

'And your whole family.' Raul didn't even try to deny it. 'You seem to bring death and destruction with you wherever you go. You ruined my chances of giving my father an heir when you walked out on me and then your brother killed my sister and the baby she was carrying.'

'It wasn't his fault!'

'It doesn't matter!'

An angry gesture with a lean brown hand dismissed the furious protest as totally irrelevant. And Raul too got to his feet in a wild, angry movement that made Alannah think nervously of the savage pounce of a wild hunting leopard leaping onto its defenceless prey.

Instinctively she took a couple of hasty steps backwards, out of his range.

'The end result is the same! My sister is dead and her baby with her.'

'So—I repeat—why? Why would you want to marry me or have anything to do with me or any member of my family?'

'Because you owe me!' Raul tossed at her, his words hissing savagely, eyes black with fury. 'You owe me a child. An heir. You and your brother destroyed my family's chances of having another generation to grow up, have our blood in their veins…'

'To inherit the Marquez Marcín dukedom—the estate…'

'That as well.' Raul shrugged off her weak-voiced protest, intent only on what he wanted.

'But—but you can't do this—you can't want to—I don't want to—I don't want you…'

'Liar!'

It was low-voiced, deadly as the strike of a serpent. And he actually laughed, throwing back his proud head to let out a crack of laughter that was so harsh, so cold, so totally without any trace of real humour in it that it made her flinch back, wincing as she seemed to feel it splintering in the air around her, sending tiny shards of ice showering over her skin.

'You know that's not true and it never has been true. That's the one thing we have going for us in this, *querida*…'

His tone turned the word into a sound that was light-years away from the endearment it was meant to be.

'We can't keep our hands off each other—never have been able to. And that's what will make this whole thing so easy—and so pleasurable.'

Alannah could only stare at him in horror, unable to believe what she was hearing.

'Easy!' was all she could say. He really thought that this could be *easy*?

'Think about it, *belleza*. From the moment we met again in that hospital, we haven't been able to stay away from each other—we never could and we still can't. I want you and you want me. No one else has ever made me burn like this. And you burn too—you can't deny it—you went up in flames in my arms—in my bed—just now. I want more of that and so, if you're honest, do you.'

When had he moved? She hadn't actually seen him take any steps towards her but suddenly he was so close. Close enough to reach out a hand and smooth warm, gentle fingertips down the side of her face. With her mind a battlefield, the mental turmoil seemed to have stopped her thought processes. She wanted to draw back, pull away from him, but somehow her body wouldn't obey the commands she thought she was giving it. Instead it reacted with the opposite of what she wanted—thought she wanted, told herself she wanted—and she angled her face into the caress like a cat that wanted to be stroked.

Raul's smile was almost gentle but threaded through with a dark triumph that caught and twisted in her soul.

'See? You can't deny it—your body won't let you. You're mine. Always were mine and always will be mine.'

She had to find the strength to fight the wicked, enticing spell he was weaving, his words curling round her like warm, perfumed smoke, drugging, intoxicating.

'No—I said no!'

With a wrench that tore at her heart she forced herself away from him, the violence of the movement taking her halfway across the room towards the door.

'This isn't going to happen. You can't expect me to marry you—not like this.'

If she looked into his face, into his eyes one more time she would swear that he could hypnotise her into agreeing, whether she wanted to or not. So she made herself take a step towards the door. And another. He let her get almost close enough to grab at the handle before he spoke again.

'Running away again, Alannah?'

The words taunted her, his mocking tone seeming to rip away strips of her skin, leaving her raw and vulnerable, totally exposed.

'You can't make me stay!' She flung it over her shoulder at him, still not daring to look round. Just one sight of his face would weaken her, finish her forever. 'You can't make me do this!'

'I might not have to. Fate may have pushed your hand. Think about it—you might already be pregnant. I didn't use any protection. We didn't have time—or the presence of mind—to consider it. Even now you might be carrying my child.'

'And if I am, then why can't I bring it up on my own? Thousands of women do so every day.'

'Thousands of women do,' Raul agreed with

stunning calm. 'But not one of them is carrying my child—my heir. Have my child without marriage and I'll fight you with every last breath in my body.'

'Then fight me! If I am pregnant—sue me, take me to court! You can't force me to marry you!'

She couldn't take any more. She had to get out of here fast before her thought processes disintegrated into a spinning mist, before she broke down completely. The door handle was solid beneath fingers that trembled so badly she felt she might never get it open. But at last she managed it and stumbled out into the corridor beyond. The walls seemed to dance before her eyes, make her feel dizzy and sick.

And still Raul hadn't finished with her.

'You can run but you'll never get away.' His voice followed her from inside the room. 'I'll come after you. I can't let you go.'

Now she really was running away, Alannah admitted to herself as she forced her unsteady feet to carry her forwards. The thundering race of her heart, the pounding of blood at her temples told her how important this all was. She was running from Raul, running from herself, running from the truth.

Because the truth was that she longed to say yes.

The truth, the appalling, the terrible but the totally undeniable truth was that she had to face up to the reality of how she was really feeling. And that truth was something that she had been avoiding for days. Ever since this man had walked back into her life.

She had told herself she hated him. And then when she hadn't been able to keep away from him, when she had fallen into bed with him in denial of self-preservation or common sense or even logic, she had tried to explain that away as overwhelming physical need. A lust so intense and concentrated that it was like some volatile explosive—light the fuse and stand well back to avoid getting caught in the red-hot lava of the fallout.

But it hadn't been the fallout that had got her. She had been right there at the centre of the explosion. Burning up in the savage heat of all that had blown up around her. And it had been where she most wanted to be. Where she needed to be. The only place she could be because it was where she belonged.

Because she still loved Raul with all her heart and nothing that had happened in the past two years had done anything to destroy that love. And now she doubted that anything ever would.

That was the reason she was here, wasn't it? She might as well admit that right from the start she had used the need to return his mobile phone as just an excuse to come here and see him one last time. She could have packed it up and put it in the mail, or had it sent round to him as he had been going to send Carlos to her flat to pick it up once he had realised it was missing. But no, she had had to bring it herself and, even as she had been denying that she ever wanted to see him again, she had been making moves that guaranteed she would have to do just that.

'We can heal our families, Alannah.'

Raul's voice sounded inside her head, all the more devastating because she knew he told the truth. This would help her mother heal. It might even save her life.

The thought of a future, of new life coming into the world where there had been so much loss and tragedy, would give her something to live for. And it would be the same for Raul's father, the old man that she had grown fond of in the short time she had known him.

And what if she *was* already pregnant?

Alannah's arms folded round her body as the thought hit home. Her stumbling footsteps slowed, halted.

She might already be carrying Raul's child.

And the sudden, devastating surge of joy that welled up inside her at just the thought told its own story. She wanted to be carrying Raul's baby. She *longed* for it to be true. Because the truth was that she loved this man so much that the thought of being pregnant with his child was something she'd always cherished.

The thought of being pregnant with his child and *married* to him.

But how could she consider marrying him when she knew he was only doing it because of the child he wanted so desperately? The much-needed heir—and the blazing, all-consuming passion that flared between them at a touch, a look. There was no denying that passion, or the need that it fired.

But was it enough?

Could a relationship survive when only one person loved and the other simply wanted?

Without realising it, she found that she had actually turned where she stood so that now she was facing back down the corridor, looking towards where the door to Raul's suite still stood open. Subconsciously it seemed that she had already made the decision.

So he only wanted her for passion and for the child he needed. At least this time she knew where she stood. He was being totally open about it all. And if she loved him and his child, and he loved his child, then surely it could be enough.

It would have to be enough because the alternative was one she couldn't live with. She couldn't face a life and a future without Raul in it.

'You can run but you'll never get away.' Raul's voice echoed inside her head. 'I'll come after you. I can't let you go.'

I can't let you go. If that was as much as she was ever going to get she'd learn to live with it.

So she walked slowly back, knowing Raul was right, she might run from him but she would always have to come back. She was at the mercy of her own love for him, a love that she could never live without. It was as essential to life itself as the beat of her heart. Without Raul she was only half a person and yet with him she could never be truly complete because the part that needed his love would always be left empty and unfulfilled, like a raw, bleeding wound. But if she walked away now then her whole life would be that way. It wasn't much of a choice but it was the only one that she had.

She'd said goodbye to him once and she had barely survived it. She had spent the next two years trying to cope without him and never managing it. Because of that she had fallen straight into his arms as soon as he had reappeared in her life. She couldn't put herself through that again. It was one thing doing it blind as she had done the first time. Making herself face it again when she knew what the agony was like was emotional suicide.

In a choice between two agonies, then the misery of knowing that Raul didn't love her was the one she could bear more than the desolation of knowing she would never, ever see him again.

She had thought that after this there was no possibility of going through anything more, that she had endured every emotional upheaval she could possibly undergo. But the dreadful thing was that as she walked back into the room it was to find that Raul was still standing exactly where he had been before. The only thing that was different was that he had folded his arms across his chest as he stood there, waiting.

Just waiting.

He hadn't troubled to take a single step after her or even try to stop her leaving.

He had known all the time that she would come back. Have to come back to him and accept his terms.

And he had just been waiting for her to do so.

CHAPTER TEN

FOUR months and not a sign of a baby.

Alannah sighed as she stared out of the window high up in the Castillo de Alcántara, her thoughts far away, her eyes not even seeing the dramatic silhouette of the Guadarrama Mountains where they rose high on the far horizon, way beyond the vineyards that gave the Marcín family so much of their wealth. When she had arrived here at the huge, sprawling, ancient *castillo* that was Raul's family home, those mountains had been tipped with snow at the skyline. But as the time had passed, and the sun had grown stronger, the snow had gradually melted and disappeared.

Now, like the snow, those terrible days in the early spring when the tragedy of the car crash had brought Raul back into her life were slipping into the past and time had started to blur the memories of how bleak and devastating the loss had been. She had learned how to move on into life again. Even her mother had seemed to find a way, as someone had once said, to live around the hole where Chris had once been.

'We can heal our families, Alannah.'

Once more Raul's words sounded inside her head and in the privacy of her thoughts she acknowledged the fact that he had been right—so right—in his assessment of the situation. From the moment that she had told her mother that Raul had asked him to marry her, that they were planning on marrying as soon as possible and trying for a baby straight away, it was as if a new spark had lit inside Helena's heart. She still grieved desperately for her beloved son, but there was a reason for living, a reason to get up every day, and she had welcomed it with open arms.

As had Raul's father, Matias. When Alannah had first arrived at the *castillo* and seen the old man for the first time in two years she had been shocked at the way that the passage of time and the shock of his personal loss had aged him, leaving him frail and unsteady on his feet, his dark eyes clouded by sorrow. He had almost wept when Raul had told him that he hoped to bring him a grandchild to hold in his arms just as soon as nature would allow it, and, seeing the tears that had sheened those eyes, so like his son's, Alannah had known that, for this reason if for nothing else, because of the new meaning her marriage would bring to these two sad, lonely people, her mother and Raul's father, she was doing the right thing.

And if by doing so she could fill her own life with the bitter-sweet delight of having Raul there with her every day, sharing his bed at night, with his beloved face the first thing she saw every morning and the last before she fell asleep at the end of the day, then she told herself that that would be enough. She would take what he would give her and not ask for more.

Or, rather, she would try not to ask for more.

But deep in her heart she knew that there was one thing she still yearned for.

Oh, not Raul's love. She wasn't such a fool as to dream of that. But he was marrying her to have a child. The longed-for grandchild for his father and her mother. The heir to all the Marcín estates.

'We can heal our families, Alannah. We can't replace what they've lost but we can offer them a future. A future with a grandchild to look forward to.'

But four months down the line, there was still no sign of the baby this marriage was all about.

And no sign of the proposed marriage either.

A cruel, icy little hand clutched at her heart at that thought. Four months ago Raul had been all fire and impatience, determined to arrange the marriage almost overnight, it seemed. But then, of course, there had been the possibility that she might already be pregnant to spur him on.

And she had hoped too.

But it seemed that no sooner had she allowed the dream to take root in her thoughts than fate had destroyed it overnight. There was to be no baby.

'Not this time,' Raul had said with unexpected calm when she had told him. 'But we would have been expecting miracles for everything to go right all at once. We have time. And we can enjoy trying again.'

Alannah sighed again and ran her finger along the

heavy stone ledge outside the open window, feeling the heat of the sun on her skin.

She wasn't sure that 'enjoy' was strictly the right word.

Oh, there was no doubt at all that she reached the heights of pleasure in Raul's arms and in his bed. Heights of pleasure that she had never imagined existed or thought that she would scale over and over again. And she knew that Raul's sexual hunger for her was every bit as sharp and as urgent as it had been from the very first. He showed no sign at all of growing bored or even indifferent now that she was in his bed every night. But at the same time he showed no sign of feeling anything more. He told her she was beautiful, murmured husky, seductive compliments in her ear as she lay under him, open to him, giving herself to him.

But never, ever did he speak a single word of love.

And so the pleasure she enjoyed always came with a feeling that it was the very sharp edge of a double-edged sword. Every time that she made love to Raul it bound her closer and closer to him than she would ever have believed possible. She had given him her heart from the start but now it seemed that he possessed her totally, body and soul, and without him she would be just an empty shell. But he made love to her to 'try again'. He came to bed with her because he wanted her, it was true, but always, always the thought of that baby they were to make between them was on his mind.

But up until now there was no sign of that longed-for child.

And no sign of the wedding either.

And if there was one way to make it painfully clear to her that Raul had only promised one as long as she delivered the other, then that was it. No baby, no wedding. He didn't have to spell it out. It was as plain as day without a word being spoken.

Savagely Alannah dashed the back of her hand against her eyes to brush away the bitter tears she didn't dare to let herself shed. If she started to cry then she feared she would never stop, and when Raul came home from Madrid where he had gone for the day, he would find her with red eyes and swollen lids and would demand to know the reason for her tears.

And she would never, ever be able to tell him.

Four months and no sign of a baby. Raul swung his car into the big stone-paved courtyard outside the *castillo* and pulled on the brake. Four months in which the whole purpose of this marriage seemed to have been put on hold—just not happening. Four months in which the much-needed heir to the Marcín dynasty had not yet made an appearance.

And it was obvious that Alannah was getting twitchy.

She always seemed to be on edge, barely able to hold a conversation with him, and not meeting his eyes when she did speak. And she often found some excuse not even to be in the same room as him. The only time and the only place where they communicated was in bed. There they had no need for words. There the simple, direct, uncomplicated bond that was the burning sexual passion they shared brought them together in complete empathy, their connection instinctive and intuitive. And the blazing fulfilment they achieved every time was simply mind-blowing.

In bed everything was perfect.

Or was it?

Getting out of the car, he opened the back door, reached in and picked up the huge bouquet of roses that lay on the back seat. Kicking the door shut again, he pressed the remote control to lock it and headed towards the big arched doorway into the *castillo*, his expression sombre, a frown drawing his dark brows together.

In bed everything was amazing. But perfect? Wasn't the truth the fact that Alannah was only so responsive, so ardent, because she was desperate to make this baby that would mean so much to her mother? The baby that was the only reason they were together.

His father was getting twitchy too, Raul acknowledged to himself as he strode up the wide stone steps and into the cool, shadowy tiled hall. Matias was anxious to know when the grandchild he wanted so much would make its appearance. And every month when the answer was, 'Not yet, Padre…' he would shake his head and mutter under his breath.

And both Matias and Alannah's mother wanted to know when the wedding would be. Why hadn't they set a date yet? What were their plans?

They didn't have plans, Raul acknowledged, heading up the stairs towards his bedroom. Alannah had showed no sign of being interested in the ceremony; she appeared to be content with things the way they were. And the truth was that so was he. More content than he had been for years. He had the woman he wanted in his home. She was there every day when he came back; she was in his bed every night.

In fact, if it wasn't for his father's age, he would have been happy to wait for the baby to come along as nature dictated.

But Alannah had agreed to have that baby only because of what it would mean to her mother and to Matias. That was her only reason for being here. And it was obvious that she was getting restless at the thought that it might never happen.

She was at the window when he entered the room, standing leaning against the wide stone sill, looking out towards the mountains on the far horizon, so absorbed that she hadn't heard him come in, and for a moment he could simply stand and watch her, acknowledging all over again the way that her unique beauty hit home afresh every time he saw her.

She was wearing a loose blue-green dress, darker than the one she had worn on the day she had come to his hotel to return his phone, and with a swirling abstract pattern on it that made him think of the depths of the sea when the sun and the shadows mixed on it. Her feet were bare, one set of pink-tipped toes that tapped restlessly on the floor the only trace of movement about her, the rest of her slender body so still that she might have been a statue carved from marble. Certainly her skin was pale enough for it, but no marble had ever had the glorious rich colour of the swathe of her hair that fell loose around her face and onto her shoulders, soft strands of it stirring gently in the faint breeze. Seeing it, he itched to bury his fingers in the silky red-gold strands, to feel them slide along his palm, breathe in the intensely personal scent of them, press his mouth against them.

The way she leaned against the sill pressed her breasts onto the ledge of her folded arms, revealing the pale curves in the scooped neckline of her dress, the soft swell of them drying his mouth with need in the space of a heartbeat. It was not even seven hours since that morning, when he had forced himself from the bed where he had made slow, deeply sensual love to her as she came awake in his arms, and yet already his body was as hungry for her as if he had been away for seven days—seven months.

'Raul?'

Some movement he had made had caught her attention. She'd turned her head to see him standing in the doorway. The moments of quiet observation, of the freedom to watch her without constraint, were gone and he was back with the puzzle that was Alannah.

'You're early.'

And she was none too pleased about it, to judge from the rough edge to her voice. She preferred to be alone and not to be troubled by his company—and yet this was the woman who could not seem to get enough of him in bed.

Just what had happened to change the sweet, free-spirited innocent he had met almost three years ago into this withdrawn and strangely distant creature? It was as if she was always holding something back, and he had no idea just what that 'something' might be.

'I wasn't expecting you yet.'

'*Buenas tardes, Alannah.*'

He pitched his voice at a carefully casual note, not wanting her to guess at any of his thoughts. Moving into the room, he dropped a swift kiss onto her soft mouth, touching her cheek briefly with his free hand.

'I couldn't stay away—I missed you.'

'Missed me?' She sounded frankly sceptical. 'You've only been away for a few hours.'

'Hours in which all I could think of was how beautiful you looked when I left you this morning—lying in my bed with your hair spread out around you on the pillows, and your skin still glowing from my love-making. I couldn't concentrate on any of the meetings I had and I drove like a maniac all the way home. I only stopped to buy these.'

'Flowers?'

Alannah stared at the huge bouquet of roses in deep, rich pink as he held them out to her. In the same moment that her heart leapt at the thought that he had bought her flowers—and such beautiful flowers—another very different feeling twisted a cruel knife deep in her already vulnerable heart as her mind went back over what he had said.

…all I could think of was how beautiful you looked when I left you this morning—lying in my bed with your hair spread out around you on the pillows, and your skin still glowing from my lovemaking.

That 'beautiful' should have delighted her but he had made no secret of how much he was attracted to her; how much he desired her. And he was still thinking of her in purely sexual terms, thinking of the slow, sensual way he had made love to her this morning as she came awake in his arms.

Sexual and deeply possessive terms: 'in *my* bed… your skin still glowing from *my* lovemaking.' He might have asked her to be his wife but she was still just a mistress in the way he thought of her. A mistress who was there to bring him pleasure at the end of his day, to warm his bed and tend to his needs. A mistress who could be discarded at any moment, if—when—he grew tired of her. If she didn't meet the terms of his proposal.

She would only become his wife when she fulfilled her part of the bargain. When she became pregnant with the baby he wanted, then and then only would he seal his part of the bargain with a wedding ring.

If only she truly was the woman he wanted as his wife, she couldn't help thinking as she glanced up into the deep set bronze eyes, seeing the way he was watching her, the faint creases at the corners of the hooded lids. If she was then this moment when he had come home early would be so special for her. She would be overjoyed to see him, would be able to run to him, throw herself into his arms, kiss him in delighted greeting. Whisper her love for him in his ear. If only…

She *was* delighted to see him. It was the rest that got in the way, holding her back from the way she really wanted to respond.

So instead she schooled her expression into polite appreciation, cooled her voice to mirror the same as she continued, 'Why have you brought me flowers?'

'Do I need a reason to bring my…to bring you flowers?'

The hesitation was tiny but it was there. And, because it came so close to the way that she had already been thinking, the slight pause, the tiny silence seemed to scrape over nerves already stretched too tight and rawly exposed.

Raul didn't know what to call her. Terms like wife or bride were not the ones that came to mind. She wasn't even truly his fiancée, though her left hand wore the ring he had insisted on giving her for form's sake, as part of the plan to help their grieving parents. Emotional words, *my love, my darling,* wouldn't even enter his mind.

So how did he think of her? Had she come closest of all with that 'mistress' she had thought of earlier? And yes, Raul might bring his *mistress* flowers. The mistress he had left in his bed that morning; the mistress he had made love to before leaving the house, and whom he anticipated making love to again just as soon as he could.

No.

There was that cruel stab of harsh reality piercing right into her soul as she forced herself to face the truth. However much Raul might call it lovemaking, even though she herself had so described what they had done here, in the big bed with the huge carved wooden headboard, no matter how many times they did it and how much pleasure he gave her—they gave each other—it was never, ever making love. There was some vital element missing, an imbalance that put all the loving on to her side of the scales and left Raul's feelings dangerously light in that area. And that turned what they did, so often and so pleasurably, into 'having sex' and never the wonder that was making love.

'No?' he questioned, a previously unheard edge in his voice. 'No, I don't need a reason or no…you don't want the flowers?'

It took her another second to realise that in the middle of her thoughts she had spoken that 'No' aloud and Raul had taken it to mean that she was talking about the flowers. And if she wasn't going to have to explain what she had really been thinking about then she had to cover her tracks pretty hastily.

'No, of course you don't need an excuse to bring me flowers. Thank you.'

It was as she moved forward to press a swift kiss of gratitude on his lean cheek that she caught the flash of something in his eyes, something that, like that note in his voice, was new and incomprehensible to her. But she didn't have time to try and decipher it because, in the minute that her lips neared his strong jaw, Raul suddenly turned his head quickly so that it was not his cheek that made contact with them but his mouth.

His hot, hungry, demanding mouth.

And it was like a match landing on bone-dry brush-wood, the spark, the flare, the flame instantaneous and wild, the roaring conflagration of need swamping them in a second, burning up thought, driving away restraint, and leaving only yearning, hotly demanding hunger in their place.

The bouquet fell from Raul's hand, finding a nearby chair instead of the floor only by good luck, not man-agement, and with his hands now free he hauled her close to him, crushed her up against him as he took her mouth in a searing, thought-obliterating kiss.

Alannah's lips opened under his, inviting him to deepen the kiss, and he followed her encouragement without hesitation, plundering her mouth, sending them spinning into a roaring hurricane of need that spun her out of reality and into a world of total sensation. She flung her arms up around his neck and gave herself up to it, putting all the need, the loneliness, the sense of loss and despair she had felt through the day into her response.

And was shocked to meet with something that in another man she would have described as just the same reaction as her own. There was a new rawness in Raul's kiss, a new urgency in the caress of his hands. It was as if he had been parted from her for days, weeks—and not just the few brief hours they had been apart.

She was swung up into his arms, carried to the bed, her clothing somehow disposed of—as was his—and all the while his mouth clung to hers—or hers to his, she had no way of knowing which—with a wild and primitive hunger that was beyond words, beyond thought, locked solely in the realms of need, of total surrender to the moment.

Their coming together was fast and furious, a lightning storm of burning passion and heated desire. And yet somehow they were also the most giving moments she had known with this man, the closest he had ever come to what she would have given the name of love-making if she had been asked. Unlike the long, slow sex of that morning, when he had indulged every sensual need he had, and given her back the same delight a thousandfold, this time had a new and—there was that word again—a very raw edge to it. One that she had never known before, and didn't understand. But she knew how it made her feel, the way it wrenched her from reality and brought her tumbling wildly out of the world, crying out his name on a sound of stunned completion as everything she knew exploded about her, shattered into tiny pieces that instinctively she knew she could never put back together in the same way again.

It was almost as if…

She lost herself before her mind could complete the sentence, dropping into a pulsing haze of oblivion from which she only recovered slowly. More slowly than ever before. It was only as her mind gradually cleared and her thoughts started to swim up to the surface of rationality once again that reality hit her savagely right in her heart.

*It was almost as if…*she had thought, knowing that then she would have completed the sentence, *It was almost as if…*he had finally realised how much he cared about her.

But that was the wild delirium talking. It was the sort of hungry fantasy that her mind had thrown at her at the height of ecstasy, when she could believe that all her dreams could possibly come true. Now she was sinking back into cold reality. And cold reality saw things so very differently.

It was almost as if he had decided that this was the end. That he had waited long enough and, as things were not going the way he had planned, then he had decided that he was going to call the whole thing off.

And after the moment of glorious delusion, the moment when she had thought things were so won-drously possible, the cruel disappointment was like a set of savage talons clawing at her heart. The anguish was all the worse because there was no way she could express it, no way she could admit to Raul that she had been foolish enough to allow herself to believe…

'What is it?' Raul had sensed her withdrawal, the change of mood that kept her distant, held her body stiffly away from his instead of cuddling close in the aftermath of ecstasy. 'Now what's wrong?'

His tone caught on the edge of painfully exposed nerves, pushing her into wild, unconsidered speech.

'I was wondering how long all this is going to go on. When it's going to end.'

Beside her he stiffened in his turn, the long, powerful body losing the indolent relaxation of fulfil-ment, every muscle tensing like those of a wild animal sensing an invader coming unwanted into its territory.

'Who says it has to end at all?'

He was half sitting now, propped up on one elbow, his head resting on one hand. Alannah knew he was looking at her but she refused to meet his eyes, staring fixedly instead straight up at the white-painted ceiling.

'Well, we both know it has to finish some time— there's nothing really to keep us together, and we both know that. I'm just a womb you're renting for nine months, and then when you're done…'

'When I'm done, *que*?' Raul murmured with a

darkly ironical edge to the question. 'When I'm done then do you think I will discard you like an empty husk, when I have enjoyed the sweetness of the nut inside the shell and sated myself on it?'

It was what she feared most so for a moment she didn't dare to answer but simply turned a furious glare in his direction. A furious, sightless glare. She didn't dare to look into his shuttered, watchful face for fear of what she might read there. She might know that she was speaking the truth but she didn't want to *see* it in his expression, read it in his eyes.

'I don't know, do I?' she said at last when he was obviously determined to wait for her to answer. 'I don't know what's going on in that head of yours. Why don't you tell me what you have planned?'

'What I have planned…'

Raul got up from the bed and wandered over to the window, staring out at the mountains on the horizon just as Alannah had done such a short time before. And now, with his long, straight back to her and with the heat of passion cooling as swiftly as the sheen of perspiration on her skin, she suddenly felt a terrible twist of fear clench in her heart as she wished the foolish question back.

'What I have planned is a wedding.'

It was the last thing she was expecting and the words swung round and round in her head, repeating themselves over and over but never making any clearer sense at all.

What I have planned is a wedding. But why? Why now? When there was no sign of the baby he was marrying her for?

Turning, he snatched up the bouquet of roses from the chair onto which they had fallen and tossed them towards her in an angry gesture, heedless of any damage he might do to the delicate petals as they landed on the bed.

'That was why I bought these. When I was in Madrid today I finalised all the arrangements. Everything is in hand and all you have to do is to choose your dress and come to the church on the right day.'

'And when is the right d-day?' Alannah stammered, totally unable to believe she was hearing right. Had he really arranged the wedding? Was he really going to marry her? Even without the baby?

'The fourteenth,' Raul told her flatly, stunning her even more. 'You have just two weeks before you become Dona Raul Marquez Marcín.'

CHAPTER ELEVEN

THE night air was still and warm after the intense heat of the day as Alannah wandered through the shadowy grounds of the *castillo*, knowing that, late as it was, there was no point at all in going back to her room. There was no way she was going to be able to sleep; not tonight.

'Get plenty of rest, darling,' had been her mother's last words to her as she kissed her goodnight. 'You want to look your very best tomorrow.'

The rest was an impossibility, Alannah knew, and as for looking her very best for the wedding—well, that wasn't something she had come to a decision about yet. And that was why she was now wandering restlessly around the moonlit grounds, trying to force herself to make up her mind. Besides, she had the miserable suspicion that if she went back and got into bed then as soon as the light was out and she was lying in the darkness the tears would start—and she was very much afraid that she wouldn't be able to make them stop.

Tomorrow was her wedding day. Within less than

fourteen hours she was expected to have done her hair and make-up, slipped into the beautiful, delicate gown that Raul had arranged for a world-famous designer to create and produce for her at the speed of light, and be ready to step into the chauffeur-driven limo, to be taken to the huge mediaeval cathedral at Léon, where Raul was waiting to take her as his bride.

And that was the problem.

How could she marry Raul when she knew he didn't love her?

For the baby, he would have said. But only this morning she had had undeniable proof that once again her body had let her down. The familiar ache low down in her pelvis had been followed, with cruel inevitability, by the arrival of her period.

Once again there was no hope of a baby very soon.

And without that hope, how could she go through a ceremony to become Raul's wife, taking vows she would mean to keep, when she knew that he would never feel the same?

She had told herself that she could do it, that she would manage to cope. But now, with the day very nearly here, the wild, whirling panic of her thoughts told her that she couldn't go through with it.

And still she had chickened out of telling him. She had let him move his things into another room for tonight, in deference to her mother's superstitious conviction that it was bad luck for the groom to see his bride before the wedding, and she had accepted his kiss with a cool equanimity that she was far from feeling. And she hadn't found the courage to even try to tell him the truth.

Now, with midnight fast approaching, everyone in the *castillo* was sound asleep, dreaming of the coming ceremony, and she was on her own, wandering miserably through the darkness, knowing that it didn't matter if Raul saw her before the wedding or not, the true bad luck had already jinxed this marriage before it had even begun.

'Couldn't you sleep either?'

The voice, low, masculine and instantly familiar, made her start as it came to her on the night air, apparently from nowhere.

'Who?'

Whirling, she stared round into the darkness in bewilderment, unable to see who had spoken.

'Raul?'

'Here.'

From the shadows under a tall tree another shadow detached itself, vague and almost invisible, Raul's black hair and black clothing blending with the darkness of the night. Only the lighter tone of his skin caught the glimmering rays of the moon, making it visible—just—as he took a couple of steps forward into the light.

'What—what are you doing here?'

There was a distinct quaver on the words, Raul noted, but just what had put it there? It was impossible to tell how she was feeling and her face, wide-eyed and desperately pale in the moonlight, gave nothing away.

Nothing except that she was in total shock at seeing him there. And that was only to be expected, after all. After they had said goodnight an hour ago she must have thought that he was safely tucked up in a bed at the opposite end of the *castillo*. Hopefully asleep, or if not then so deep in his own preparations for tomorrow that he would never notice she had set out on a midnight ramble.

'I came to find you.'

'But…'

Alannah pushed one hand through the tumble of soft hair, its colour drained by the bluish light of the moon, and he would have to have been totally blind not to see the way it shook, the effort she was having to make to try to control her reaction.

So was it a response to him that made her feel this way—or the knowledge of what she had planned?

Whatever she did have planned. Just for a moment his fingers touched the pocket of his jeans where a small sheet of folded paper was hidden. She didn't know that he had it in his possession, and he wasn't going to let her know, not until he had some better idea of just what was going on inside her lovely head.

'Why—how did you know I was here?' Alannah managed, every stumble of her tongue, every abruptly broken-off word setting his teeth on edge even more. Did she not know how much she was giving away— the way she was making it blatantly obvious that something was very wrong?

But what? One part of him wanted to push him into demanding to know right away, to get her to tell him *now* before he went out of his mind with impatience. But another, more rational part, warned him to wait, to take his time to find out and not to rush her into saying something he might not want to know.

'I came to your room. I wanted to talk to you, but as your mother had set a careful curfew I didn't get a chance until she had gone to bed.'

Somehow he managed to inject a lightness into his voice that he was very far from feeling and, hearing it, he saw her relax slightly, her tense shoulders dropping, her clenched fingers loosening.

'What did you want to talk to me about?'

'Let's walk a little before I tell you. There's something I want you to see.'

She fell into step beside him as he set off along the path, walking alongside, but just keeping enough distance so that he would have to make a real thing of reaching for her hand if he wanted to hold it.

He decided to leave that for now. He didn't want to make a real thing of it—not till he found out more. Once again his fingers brushed over his pocket, hearing the faint crackle of the paper inside.

'Where are we going?'

She still sounded edgy; worse than ever, in fact, though she was trying very hard to erase the tension from her voice.

'Not very far. In fact—here we are.'

'Here?'

This time it was blank bewilderment that sounded in the word. He could see her eyes flashing faintly as she looked around for something that he might have brought her to see.

'What…?'

Raul lifted one booted foot and rested it on the hollow trunk of a fallen tree that lay almost hidden by the side of the path.

'This. I wanted you to see my special place. This was where I used to come and sit when I was a kid—still do now. It was also where I hid when things went wrong.'

Stooping, he peered down into the darkness of the huge hole inside the trunk.

'Believe it or not I could get in there once. I wouldn't like to try it now.'

He watched the play of emotions flit across her face, wariness fading into amusement, understanding and finally into uncertainty. And it was uncertainty that held when she looked up at him as he straightened again.

'I hid in there when they came to tell me that Rodrigo had died.'

She had been about to speak but his words stopped her dead. Twice she opened her mouth and both times she closed it again without managing to make a sound. But he knew the question she wanted to ask.

'He was my brother.'

That brought a gasp, a shake of her head as if in disbelief.

'I didn't know.'

'My father never wanted anyone to speak about him. When we lost him, it was as if he had never existed. He caught meningitis and no one realised in time. He was only ill for a couple of days.'

'How—how old was he?'

'Just six. And I was four.'

'You were the younger brother! But I thought…'

'You thought that I was always the heir to all this…'

With one lean brown hand he gestured to take in all the land that surrounded them, the darkened *castillo* in the distance.

'But no. I was the second son—until Rodrigo died. Then I took on the role—and I was always taught that it was my duty to provide another heir…'

He had hoped that that would help her understand. But whatever reaction he had expected, it was not the one he got. Instead Alannah flung up her hands before her face and whirled away as if in shock.

'Oh, no! No! That's not going to happen. I can't go through with this…I can't! Raul, I am not going to marry you!'

So it was as bad as he'd thought. Worse. He'd feared as much since he had gone to her room and found it empty. It was as he'd been about to turn, to go to hunt for her somewhere else, that he'd seen the single sheet of paper on the writing desk. And his name at the top.

'Dear Raul…I'm sorry…'

'OK…'

He forced himself to pitch it at calm and indifferent, almost throw-away. He wasn't going to make this any harder than it had to be.

Harder for her. He'd known it was coming, so he could handle it—for now. And then when she'd gone—as it was obvious that she was going to go now…

OK?

OK?

Alannah couldn't believe what she was hearing. She felt as if her heart was going to burst from the pain of that single word, the supreme indifference with which Raul threw it at her. She'd told him that she was not going to marry him—that she couldn't—and all he could say was…

OK.

She'd always known that he didn't love her, but she had thought that his desire for her might merit more than that. His desire for her, and his desire for a Marcín heir, the desire she now understood so much more than ever before—surely they would at least have made him raise a protest? Made him command her to stay, declare as he once had that he wouldn't let her go?

No. Memory came back to her in a rush, amending that line, changing a single word. And it seemed that that single word made all the difference in the world.

'You can run but you'll never get away.' Raul's voice echoed inside her head. 'I'll come after you. I can't let you go.'

I *can't* let you go.

Not I won't let you go—but I can't…

It was as if someone had just rewired her brain and suddenly she was looking back, seeing things she'd never seen before, making connections…

She had heard that tone of voice before. Two weeks ago. In their room. On the day that he had brought her the roses.

'Raul,' she said slowly, still thinking, still working it out, 'why did you feel you had to buy me roses?'

She had thought he might not follow her but apart from a quick frown there was no hesitation. He understood the time that she meant.

'Because I was going to tell you that I'd arranged the wedding—and I didn't feel that I had to. I wanted to.'

'You'd never bought me flowers before.'

'I know.'

He pushed his hands deep into his pockets, paced the length of the hollow tree trunk, shoulders hunched as if against some burden that had suddenly fallen on them. At the end of the tree he paused, turned back to face her. In the moonlight his face was pale and set into rigid, defensive lines.

Defensive lines.

'And that was the whole point. I wanted to try and start again. Do the whole damn proposal over again. Go down on one knee if need be—and give you the flowers…'

Something in her face had alerted him, made him aware of just what he was saying. He ground to a halt, clamping his mouth tight shut over what he had been about to say next.

'Oh, Raul, please! Please don't stop there! It was just getting interesting!'

'No.'

It was a low, angry growl but she could hear the way that it was coming ragged at the edges and she decided she could take the risk of trying to ignore it. If she was wrong, then she had nothing left to lose after all. But if she was right then she had everything to win.

'Yes!' she said, praying she sounded more determined than she actually felt.

Moving quickly to his side, she caught his hand and drew him down with her until they were both sitting on the log.

'Yes. You have to tell me what you were going to say—it's important.'

Was it just the effect of the moonlight or were there deep shadows in his eyes that she had never seen there before? She could only wait and see and pray that if they were there then they meant what she hoped they did.

'You were going to go down on one knee…' she prompted when he still hesitated and for one terrible moment she thought that he wasn't going to let her push him.

But then abruptly he seemed to come to a decision. The broad shoulders lifted in a dismissive shrug and he started to speak, slowly at first but then gathering pace until the words were tumbling out of him in a hurrying stream.

'I was going to ask you to marry me all over again—but properly this time. I would have gone down on one knee if I needed to—begged you to marry me if I'd needed to.'

'Because of…' Alannah began but the wild, almost desperate shake of his dark head made her break off hastily, knowing that what was to come was vitally important.

'Not just because of the baby, or our families, but for me—because I couldn't live without you. I love you—I've always loved you, right from the start. Even when I thought I hated you for walking out on me, I knew it wasn't the truth. It was still love but love that got messed up, twisted along the way. I didn't want things to go on as they were with your believing I only wanted you for sex or because I had to provide my father with an heir. It had to be because I wanted you here, beside me, for the rest of my life.'

He couldn't be aware of how tightly he was squeezing her hand, Alannah thought. He just couldn't know how his strength was almost crushing her fingers. And she welcomed the small discomfort because it was eloquent evidence of the way he was feeling—the emotion that gripped him.

'And I messed it up by turning on you—telling you I thought you only wanted…'

She couldn't finish the sentence but she knew that Raul didn't need her to.

'It didn't work out that time, but I thought it didn't matter—damn it, I was going to marry you anyway. I could wait a couple of weeks and then tell you when you were my wife. But tonight I found I couldn't wait. With the wedding so close, I knew I couldn't stand before the altar and put my ring on your finger without knowing why you were marrying me. I had to know. And so I came to your room…'

With a sigh he raked his free hand through his hair. And suddenly Alannah knew just what had happened. She had started to write him a note explaining the way she felt, the fact that she believed she had to break off their wedding plans, but then, knowing it would be cowardly to tell him in a letter, she had abandoned it barely started and come out into the gardens to try to nerve herself to tell him face to face. And that was where Raul had found her.

'You saw the letter.'

He nodded silently, reaching into his pocket and

pulling out the folded sheet of paper. Still holding on to her hand, he shook it open, spread it on his knee in the moonlight.

"'Dear Raul…I'm sorry…'" he read aloud and the unconcealed break in his voice went straight to her heart like an arrow, making her twist her fingers in his so that now she was holding his hand, and she was the one squeezing tight.

'I'm afraid I will never be able to give you a baby,' she said, her voice just a thin whisper, so low that he had to bend his head to hers to hear it, the movement bringing his forehead to rest against hers as his eyes burned down into her tear-filled ones. 'We've tried for these months and today—I—we—not this time once again…' she finished, the words breaking on a sob.

'And you think that I care?' he asked her, deep and strong and so openly sincere that there was no room for doubt in her mind. 'And why would you think it would be your fault? The problem could just as easily be mine—if there is a problem. Yes, I would love to give my father and your mother that grandchild they both want. It would mean so much to me—but what would mean more is to have your love. If I had that then I know I could handle anything.'

'And you have it—my love—you have my heart and everything that's in it. I love you Raul, I love you more than I can say…'

'Then don't try to say it…' he murmured, moving closer so that the words were spoken against her lips. 'Just kiss me—show me how you feel.'

'There's nothing I'd want more.'

She gave herself up to his kiss, feeling his arms close round her, holding her tight. She was held against the strength of his chest, hearing the strong, steady beat of his heart, and tears of joy burned in her eyes with the knowledge of all the love that was in that heart— in his strong, dependable, honourable masculine heart—for her.

She didn't know how long they stayed there, lost in each other's kisses, occasionally murmuring soft words but most of the time knowing that no words were necessary. They had come home. They had reached the point where they were not two separate people but one whole—united and ready to move into their future together.

But at long last Raul stirred reluctantly, dropping one last kiss on her smiling mouth before pushing back his shirtsleeve and glancing at his watch.

'Five to midnight,' he told her softly. 'If we're quick, we might just make it back to the house before midnight strikes and your mother's dreadful superstition comes into force.'

'I want to stay here, like this,' Alannah protested. 'I don't believe in superstition.'

'And neither do I, *querida*,' Raul said, getting to his feet and pulling her with him. 'But in this case, I will make an exception. Tomorrow I am going to marry you and I want to take no risks; this time I want everything to be perfect. Tomorrow we start the rest of our life together—so we can sacrifice just a few minutes to superstition to make sure nothing spoils it. Besides...'

He cupped her face in both his hands, looking

deeply into her eyes, pressing another lingering kiss on her mouth with the promise of more to come in that lifetime they had ahead of them. 'You need to get some sleep—because tomorrow you have a wedding to go to. And I promise you that from then on sleep will be the last thing on our minds.'

And, wrapping his arms tight around her, holding her close against his side, he turned to walk with her back to the castillo and into their future.

Celebrate 100 years of pure reading pleasure with Mills & Boon®

To mark our centenary, each month we're publishing a special 100th Birthday Edition. These celebratory editions are packed with extra features and include a FREE bonus story.

Now that's worth celebrating!

4th January 2008

The Vanishing Viscountess by Diane Gaston
With FREE story The Mysterious Miss M
This award-winning tale of the Regency Underworld launched Diane Gaston's writing career.

1st February 2008

Cattle Rancher, Secret Son by Margaret Way
With FREE story His Heiress Wife
Margaret Way excels at rugged Outback heroes…

15th February 2008

Raintree: Inferno by Linda Howard
With FREE story Loving Evangeline
A double dose of Linda Howard's heady mix of passion and adventure.

Don't miss out! From February you'll have the chance to enter our fabulous monthly prize draw. See special 100th Birthday Editions for details.

www.millsandboon.co.uk

FREE!

4 Books
and a surprise gift!

We would like to take this opportunity to thank you for reading this Mills & Boon® book by offering you the chance to take FOUR more specially selected titles from the Modern™ series absolutely FREE! We're also making this offer to introduce you to the benefits of the Mills & Boon® Reader Service™—

- ★ FREE home delivery
- ★ FREE gifts and competitions
- ★ FREE monthly Newsletter
- ★ Exclusive Reader Service offers
- ★ Books available before they're in the shops

Accepting these FREE books and gift places you under no obligation to buy, you may cancel at any time, even after receiving your free shipment. Simply complete your details below and return the entire page to the address below. You don't even need a stamp!

YES! Please send me 4 free Modern books and a surprise gift. I understand that unless you hear from me, I will receive 6 superb new titles every month for just £2.99 each, postage and packing free. I am under no obligation to purchase any books and may cancel my subscription at any time. The free books and gift will be mine to keep in any case.

P8ZEF

Ms/Mrs/Miss/Mr ....Initials................................

BLOCK CAPITALS PLEASE

Surname ....

Address ....

....

....Postcode ....

Send this whole page to:
UK: FREEPOST CN81, Croydon, CR9 3WZ

Offer valid in UK only and is not available to current Mills & Boon® Reader Service™ subscribers to this series. Overseas and Eire please write for details.. We reserve the right to refuse an application and applicants must be aged 18 years or over. Only one application per household. Terms and prices subject to change without notice. Offer expires 31st May 2008. As a result of this application, you may receive offers from Harlequin Mills & Boon and other carefully selected companies. If you would prefer not to share in this opportunity please write to The Data Manager, PO Box 676, Richmond, TW9 1WU.

Mills & Boon® is a registered trademark owned by Harlequin Mills & Boon Limited.
Modern™ is being used as a trademark. The Mills & Boon® Reader Service™ is being used as a trademark.